Chicken and Egg

Who pays the price?

Clare Druce is co-founder of Chickens' Lib, a non-violent pressure group campaigning for the abolition of cruel, intensive methods of poultry keeping.

Chicken and Egg

Who pays the price?

CLARE DRUCE

Introduction by
Richard Adams

Green Print
an imprint of The Merlin Press
10 Malden Road, London NW5 3HR

Copyright © 1989 Clare Druce
First published in 1989.
ISBN 1 85425 028 0

All rights reserved. No part of this publication may be reproduced, stored in a retrieval system, or transmitted, in any form or by any means, electronic, mechanical, photocopying, recording or otherwise, without the prior permission, in writing, of the publisher.

Typeset by Input Typesetting Ltd, London

Printed in Guildford, England by Biddles Ltd.

Druce, Clare
Chicken and egg
1. Poultry. Intensive production
I. Title
363.5

ISBN 1-85425-028 0

Contents

	Introduction by Richard Adams	vii
1	Battery Egg Production	1
2	The Broiler Chicken Industry	13
3	Intensive Egg and Chicken Production and the Law	25
4	The Role of the Ministry of Agriculture, Fisheries and Food	43
5	The Backlash	55
6	A Better Future	73
	References	98

Modern civilization can survive only if it begins again to educate the heart, which is the source of wisdom; for modern man is now far too clever to survive without wisdom.

Fritz Schumacher

Introduction

'Sir, all the arguments which are brought to represent poverty as no evil, shew it to be evidently a great evil. You never find people labouring to convince you that you may live very happily upon a plentiful fortune.' It would be vastly encouraging to hear Dr. Johnson (who hated cruelty to animals) let loose upon the subject of battery and broiler fowls. Cruel? It is perfectly obvious that it is cruel, callous to a startling degree. Who are the people who do these things? Have they no self-respect? They had once, but find they can make more money without. And, of course, keep it all under wraps as much as possible.

The evil, perhaps, may be more accurately defined as irresponsible, callous indifference. It is plain enough that the hens – deprived of living space, of movement, of anything like a natural life-span – must suffer, but it is convenient and profitable to ignore this, and to try to stop the public thinking about it. 'Well we all exploit animals, don't we?' 'Hens are silly creatures.' 'What are you going to do for hens and eggs otherwise?' Nevertheless, consciousness of the infamy won't go away: most people have it ticking away inside them somewhere.

Humanitarian reforms always cost money and are always due to the urgings of communal self-respect. To abolish black slavery cost a great deal financially, as did the abolition of child labour in factories. To-day, we find the furriers arguing that to abolish their cruel trade will cost jobs. Of course it will: jobs no longer consistent with the self-respect of decent people.

Read this book. Don't say to yourself, 'Yes, of course it's dreadful, but it's nothing to do with me.' It is. It is at present condoned by law in this country, which is a democracy with freedom of speech and of the press. So it is the electorate's communal responsibility. It is morally wrong. What are you going to do about it?

Richard Adams

Chapter 1
Battery Egg Production

'One of my jobs was removing dead birds. There was never any shortage. Due to poor light the bottom two tiers of cages were in darkness, and it was impossible to see if the birds were still alive. When the carcases were removed it was often a matter of a skeleton head and a few bones. I once took part in the clearance of a ten thousand bird shed. Other lads were brought in from local farms and the torture commenced. I recall being shouted at for my gentleness. Birds were dragged from the cages by their legs. Four birds were carried in each hand end down, down the shed to the door. The noise was deafening, the smell was putrid. Legs, wings and necks were snapped without concern. As I now look back, the whole system is incredibly cruel. After saying all this, this particular farm was good as far as battery farms go. The floors were swept daily and precautions taken against disease and pests . . . I gave up work in the poultry industry after bad dreams at night.'

Ex poultry industry worker

The egg industry is in crisis. For decades it has striven to provide consumers with a fresh, uniform commodity, free from seasonal shortages and bad eggs, yet in recent years egg sales have been in steady decline. Changing eating habits and health scares about cholesterol levels in eggs have depressed the market, to the extent that in Spring 1988 producers were selling at 29p a dozen while production costs ran at over 45p.[1] Then on 3 December Edwina Currie, junior Health Minister until her resignation some two weeks after that date, dealt the industry a body blow. In a television interview she expressed the view that 'most of the egg production in this country, sadly, is now infected with salmonella.' Within days, egg sales plummetted by up to 70%, and what was described by an informed official as a 'hellish row' broke out between the Ministries of Agriculture and Health. But underlying the vagaries of the egg market is another, more fundamental issue. The debate about the morality of keeping hens in cages is now bitter, passionate and worldwide.

How did the laying hen, traditionally a picturesque part of every farmyard, come to lose her freedom? Why, in the 1980s, is 90% of the UK's national flock of layers incarcerated behind bars?

Many diseases which threaten poultry health are spread by contact with the birds' own faeces and in the early part of this century poultry experts reasoned that if laying hens could be permanently separated from their droppings, many diseases would be eliminated. Cages with wire floors, which allowed the faeces to drop through, were designed and arranged in tiers, or batteries, to make the best use of space within the building. At first, birds were kept one to a cage, so farmers could identify the good layers, but later this was found to be uneconomic and today a typical battery cage measures 18" by 20" (45cm by 50cm) and houses five hens – for life. Battery cages came into commercial use in the 1930s, gradually gaining in popularity until by the 1970s 96% of all UK laying hens were caged. The major, and tragic, error in this development was that no account was taken of the behavioural needs of the species, and hens came to be regarded as an industrial asset, a kind of egg machine.

Other factors contributing to today's unacceptable situation have been the undoubted encouragement given to battery farmers by the Ministry of Agriculture, the willingness of veterinarians to support the system, and the tendency of consumers to turn a blind eye to the way in which their food is produced. But more of this in later chapters.

MASS EXTERMINATION OF DAY-OLD CHICKS

Most battery farmers keep their hens for the first, most productive year only. The ugly side of egg production (equally true for free range systems) begins on day one, when around 50% of all chicks that struggle free of their shells are exterminated. (In fact, MAFF defines the term 'day-old' as covering birds up to 72 hours old, so some male chicks may achieve a lifetime of three days.)[2] The reason for the killing of approximately 45 million chicks annually in the UK is that birds of the laying strain are lean, and not considered suitable for meat, so only the egg producing females are wanted. MAFF recommends disposal by gassing with 100% carbon dioxide (as opposed to less 'humane' methods such as suffocation, drowning or direct contact with the irritant liquid carbon tetrachloride, all methods frowned on by MAFF, but clearly in use at some time).[3] They warn that death may not supervene for five to ten minutes, and it seems unlikely that, as claimed by MAFF,[4] 'little or no distress' is felt by the suffocating chicks, or that the procedure is fool-proof. Cases have been reported of 'dead' chicks, bought as feed for captive animals, reviving and living to maturity.

The female chicks are reared either on deep litter or in cages, being transferred to laying cages when about eighteen weeks old. Some rearing cages adapt to take adult birds, and MAFF calls these 'day-old to death cages'.[5] In some respects chicks reared on litter are more unfortunate than cage-reared ones, experiencing as they must the trauma of being confined after tasting some degree of freedom. I have watched a newly caged pullet making frantic attempts to escape from her prison.

DISEASES OF INTENSIFICATION IN BATTERY HENS

Pullets start laying at around twenty weeks, and the majority of hens are slaughtered one year later. These birds, which should be in their prime – hens live on average for five to six years, some much longer – are described in the industry as 'spent' or 'end of lay', and indeed their condition by the time they reach slaughter age is often suggestive of geriatric concentration camp victims. Battery hens may be free from the parasitic infestations that the early battery farmers sought to overcome, but 'diseases of intensification' have taken their place. Cage layer fatigue (brittle bones with paralysis), fatty livers, egg laying problems and tumours plague battery hens, while infectious conditions such as bronchitis can spread like wildfire in the hot conditions within units where 30,000 birds or more may be kept together in one building. Vaccination programmes abound, but diseases continue to take their toll with mortality running at around 6%. Free range hens can, of course, suffer from a variety of diseases, but the battery system has ensured a whole range of diseases and painful conditions *directly caused* by the system.

'LIFESTYLE' OF THE BATTERY HEN

Various patterns of lighting are being experimented with to induce optimum profitability, but in most batteries the hen's 'day' lasts for some seventeen hours, during which time she stands on a sloping wire floor, the gradient allowing eggs to roll away for collection. For the remaining seven hours, lights are off and she must rest, crouching on the same bare, harsh surface. Frequently, battery hens' feet become deformed and injured. Food and water are supplied at the front of cages; MAFF recommends a 4″ trough space per bird.[6] The feed is monotonous, and recent research indicates that its unsuitable composition leads to painful mouth ulcers in a huge percentage of battery hens.[7] Despite attempts in recent years to improve lighting systems, most birds, especially those in the lower cages, live out their lives in a twilight underworld of gloom and shadows. Usually cages are arranged in banks, or tiers, three or four high, but ultra-modern units now boast up to eight tiers, with catwalks to facilitate inspection.

Hens in cages on the third or fourth tiers are notoriously difficult to inspect, since feed troughs obscure all but their feet and heads. Around two and a half million battery hens die every year in the UK, many succumbing in their cages to agonising conditions such as egg peritonitis, which can go unnoticed in the gloom and obscurity of a battery shed. Ascites, a disease resulting in abnormal accumulation of body fluids in the abdominal cavity, is 'very often found to be associated with tumour formation, either with single, large tumours within the cavity, or perhaps of more importance, with the multiple malignant tumours to be seen in many spent hens'.[8]

THE 'VICES' CAUSED BY DEPRIVATION

Because of the extreme confinement and barren nature of their surroundings battery hens are denied the fulfilment of almost all their age-old behavioural patterns, yet if released from their caged existence they will dustbathe, spread their wings and enjoy the warmth of the sun. I have watched a hen who had spent two years in cages build a nest within twenty-four hours of her release. Carefully gathering wisps of straw in her beak she built the nest higher and higher until almost enveloped, seemingly revelling in the experience which had been denied her for so long.

Supporters of the battery system claim that the modern hybrid hen has adapted to cage life. In fact she has merely proved her ability to live on, despite the most severe deprivations. But she more than pays the price for her tenacity, developing, and becoming the victim of, what the poultry industry terms 'vices' – feather pecking and cannibalism, symptoms of the birds' frustration and distress. Creatures whose nature it is to move around almost ceaselessly during the hours of daylight must, if severely restricted, somehow substitute their desire to peck and scratch around in the ground for grubs, worms, seeds and grasses. The only source of interest left to caged birds is the feathers, combs and flesh of their fellow cage-mates. Aled Griffiths, Chairman of the British Egg Information Council, claims (reported in *Poultry World*, September 1988) that cages 'help prevent aggression', but MAFF finds it necessary to warn battery farmers that 'the higher the light intensity . . . the greater the risk of cannibalism and the birds becoming flighty'.[9] And 'When an outbreak of vice occurs it should be tackled immediately by appropriate changes in the system of management, for example, by reduction of the lighting intensity'.[10] If the birds 'misbehave', they must be plunged into deeper gloom.

Feather pecking and bullying occur on free range, but in a well managed unit they rarely lead to serious physical damage or mortality. In cages there is no escape, and many battery hens nearing the end of their laying season retain few of their feathers, while others have become victims of cannibalism. MAFF officials often claim that these almost naked hens are in a natural moult, but this is not true, since they frequently display severe feather loss when only half way through their laying season, and many de-feathered ex-battery hens take several weeks, or even months to regain their plumage, which is not the case after a natural moult.

To minimise economic losses from feather pecking, which in its severest form leads to cannibalism, many battery farmers practise beak trimming. This mutilation is usually inflicted on chicks of 0–10 days old, or on adult birds if serious outbreaks of aggression occur. The process itself is crude in the extreme. A red-hot blade removes part of the beak and cauterises the exposed tissue in one operation, and some birds die from bleeding and shock. Feeding can be adversely affected, and recent research shows that debeaked birds may be left in a state of chronic and perhaps permanent discomfort, suffering in the same way that human amputees can from 'phantom limb pain'.[11] The Ministry of Agriculture salves its conscience by recommending that beak trimming is carried out only as 'a last resort'[12] and Aled Griffiths wrote in February '88 that '. . . beak trimming . . . rarely occurs in battery farming.'[13] However, millions of battery hens are de-beaked every year in the UK, many of them routinely, at the hatchery stage. Until 1987 all battery hens at MAFF's own Experimental Husbandry Farm at Gleadthorpe in Nottinghamshire were debeaked, an example to visiting farmers and students eager to learn the latest and best techniques.

ONLY HAPPY HENS LAY EGGS?

Another piece of false information circulated by intensive egg farmers is that 'only happy hens lay eggs'. Egg laying is a sexual/biological function in no way connected with contentment. Unless birds have suffered shock or severe illness they will continue to lay for several years, as long as suitably-balanced food is available and lights are on for enough hours to simulate the natural laying season. Light passes into the eye, causing a message to reach the brain which in turn passes its own message to the pituitary gland which produces hormones which stimulate the ovary – nothing to do with happiness! Those concerned for the welfare of hens are often accused of anthropomorphism (the attributing of human characteristics to non-human animals) but in fact this is the province of factory farmers.

One is on record as saying that in the summer months, when he leaves the battery shed doors open, his battery hens experience 'the nearest thing to heaven'. Ted Kirkwood, NFU spokesman on poultry matters and himself a battery farmer, described a battery hen's day in the following words: '. . . once the hen has pecked about she'll walk to the back of the cage, settle down and have another rest. If she fancies an egg is in the offing she will stand up to lay . . . then she sits down again, and she can preen a little bit if she wants to do, but generally all they want to do is just sit back and watch the world go by. They've all the other hens in the cage, they're all talking, you can tell by the noise they're making if they're happy . . .'[14]

One of the worst sufferings endured by the battery hen is the anxiety she feels at egg-laying time. Pre-egg-laying behaviour can last an hour or more. Under natural conditions hens seek seclusion, attend to the nest (re-arranging the nesting material if needs be) and settle to a time of quiet concentration, resenting and fearing any disturbance. Such behaviour clearly echoes the instinctive actions of earlier generations of birds, when the survival of the species depended on circumspect nesting habits. The battery hen has no scope for the fulfilment of these basic instincts and shows her frustration by anxious pacing and outbursts of aggression. The modern hybrid hen can lay up to three hundred eggs in a year (a staggering output compared with the one or two clutches of around a dozen eggs produced by her distant ancestor, the Burmese Jungle Fowl) so the egg-laying process, described by Konrad Lorenz as the worst torture to which the battery hen is exposed, is undergone almost daily. (Having no knowledge of the fate awaiting them, hens continue to form eggs right up to the time of slaughter. To avoid wasting any profitable part of the end-of-lay hen's body, eggs are removed from dead hens, despite the fact that such eggs may be 'abnormal in shape, variable in size and contaminated with permutations of blood smears, faecal material, drip marks and feathers'.[15] Such eggs, known in the trade as 'pulled' eggs, may be legally used in the manufacture of biscuits, cakes and so on. They may not, however, be sold direct to the public as shell eggs. In 1987 West Yorkshire trading standards officers uncovered an illegal trade in pulled eggs, and as a result a Keighley butcher was fined for retailing them in his shop.

FORCED MOULTING

Many battery farmers keep their flocks for a second year of lay, forcing their hens to moult quickly by a method known as forced, or induced, moulting. Some free range farmers force moult too. The procedure involves shocking the birds into a sudden moult by means of reducing the hours of light and feeding a low protein ration, for a period of fourteen days, then gradually returning 'day' length to normal. According to MAFF the objective of induced moulting is 'to give the bird a short rest from egg production, to induce the loss of excess body weight and to renew feathers . . . The complete replacement of all feathers is not essential, however good feathering will reduce energy requirement and hence feed intake in the second production period.'[16] Hens living an outdoor life with no artificial lighting to encourage them to lay would start to moult as the days shorten and go 'off lay', for a period of two to three months, returning to normal egg production as the days lengthen. In the days before battery houses and electrically-lit free range units, eggs were preserved in a solution of waterglass for use when hens were 'off lay'.

In its booklet *Poultry Technical Information No 13*, MAFF's Agricultural Development and Advisory Service (ADAS) recommended for day two of the forced moult: 'No food, light or water. Make sure the food troughs are really empty, clean out any remaining mash, collect eggs then turn off the water and light and leave the birds for 24 hours.' Chickens' Lib pointed out, in a letter to MAFF dated 22 March 1983, that this advice would encourage farmers to break the law, since the Welfare of Livestock (Intensive Units) Regulations (more of which in chapter 3) require that the stock in intensive livestock establishments is inspected 'thoroughly' at least once a day. Chris Mason of MAFF's Animal Health Division replied: 'We are grateful for this point being raised and it has been drawn to the attention of my ADAS colleagues. They have informed me that steps are being taken to ensure that future advisory publications are not deficient in specifying the requirement for inspection.'[17] When the (undated) booklet No 13 was published, considerations of welfare could hardly have been further from the minds of those responsible for its production. For example, under the heading 'Problems' it is stated: 'Whilst it is essential to restrict food intake to obtain a lean healthy layer this must not be overdone particularly in cold weather since over restriction will retard return to egg production.' No mention of the misery that would be endured by featherless, hungry hens.

The revised Codes of Recommendations for Domestic Fowls (leaflet 703, dated 1987) suggests that hens with no access to natural daylight should be given at least eight hours lighting per day. While the Codes are not mandatory, failure to observe their recommendations would 'tend to establish the guilt' of anyone accused of an offence under the Agricultural (Miscellaneous Provisions) Act 1968. So, in effect, farmers practising old-style forced moulting are running the risk of increasing their chances of prosecution, should they fall foul of the law. MAFF's more welfare orientated attitude annoyed John Farrant, editor of *Poultry World*, who wrote in March 1988: 'Humans happily pay to lose weight on expensive diets on health farms, so is it so bad for a hen to shed some surplus fat in preparation for a second laying cycle?' In an attempt to improve the image

CHICKENS' LIB

**P O BOX 2
HOLMFIRTH
HUDDERSFIELD HD7 1QT**

Tel: Huddersfield (0484) 861814 and 683158

*Patrons: The Bishop of Salisbury, The Rt. Rev. John Austin Baker. Brigid Brophy.
Margaret Lane (Countess of Huntingdon). Richard D. Ryder.*

With Compliments

of forced moulting the practice is now referred to in the industry as a 'laying pause'. Thus does the pressure of public opinion slowly bring about change.

THE END OF THE LIFE SENTENCE

Most battery hens, though, are considered 'spent' after their first year of lay. Gangs of catchers come, usually at night, and wrench the birds from their cages. Old-style cage doors may open inwards, causing extra stress and injury to the birds. Sometimes limbs are torn off, and claws left behind, entangled with the wire mesh of the cage floors. Roughly, the redundant hens are loaded on to crates and transported for slaughter at processing plants which may be many miles away. Acclimatised to a constant temperature of around 70 degrees in the battery, they may now be destined to travel through blizzards, perhaps to wait at the slaughter house for several hours, without even the benefit of protective feathers.

Hens which have been caged for a year or more develop brittle bones through lack of exercise. This fact has been appreciated for nearly half a century, yet only now is the condition and possible cure (obvious to some!) being investigated with any sense of urgency. Drs. N. G. Gregory and L. J. Wilkins of Bristol's AFRC Institute of Food Research have shown that by the time over 3,000 sample end-of-lay hens from twenty separate units were slaughtered and processed '98% of the carcases had broken bones, and on average they had six broken bones each.'[18] But even before the birds reach the waterbath stunner 29% of battery hens suffer from broken bones, most damage being caused during catching and when they are shackled on the slaughter line, though some breakages are of long standing. In birds removed from their cages in a 'non-commercial' fashion (that is, gently) the incidence of broken bones was halved. Since most catching is rough and ready in the extreme, we can assume that something approaching one third of all battery hens suffer the agony of broken bones during the hours between catching and slaughter. Horrifically, the Welfare of Poultry (Transport) Order 1988 sets no time limit on the journey to, or time spent awaiting, slaughter.

In addition to the millions of 'spent' hens which arrive at processing plants with broken bones, large numbers are found to have tumours. An official veterinary surgeon (that is, a vet officially appointed by MAFF to work on a regular basis at a slaughter house) told me that he sees a 'tremendous number' of tumours in end-of-lay hens. Viral cancer has long been recognised as a disease in poultry, but, given its contagious nature, it seems reasonable to assume that its spread is encouraged by the unhealthy intensive conditions found in factory farms. An estimated 1–2% of all birds fail to survive the journey, dying from suffocation, heat stress, cold or shock. Known as 'smothers', these victims of the system are logged as DOA (dead on arrival).[19]

Birds which should be in their prime are routinely reduced, by humankind, to something which is grotesque to contemplate, while boredom, fear and stress have been their lot.

Slaughtered battery hens rarely re-emerge in recognisable form, their pathetic carcases being processed into soups, pies, stock cubes, restaurant meals and baby foods. The massive incidence of their brittle and broken bones poses a problem for the food industry, because of the danger of bone splinters reaching the consumer. Much bone damage is inflicted by the strength of the electric shock given to stun the birds before their necks are cut. A widely adopted solution is to lower the voltage, which results in many 'old' battery hens remaining fully conscious until the bitter end.

Chapter 2
The Broiler Chicken Industry

(Broiler – a young chicken suitable or specially reared for boiling or roasting. Broiler house – a building for rearing chickens in close confinement. The Oxford Paperback Dictionary.)

'Broilers are raised on deep litter in large undivided houses. In addition to the control of temperature and ventilation and the provision of alarm and emergency standby arrangements, which are common to all animal housing, the main technical problem is the correct management of litter. There are fewer behavioural problems with these younger birds, and the main potential risk to welfare lies in the possibility of too high stocking density. We received no evidence that this was prevalent or that the recommendations of the code are inadequate.' (First Report from the House of Commons Agriculture Committee, Session 1980–81, which investigated animal welfare in poultry, pig and veal calf production.)

The fact that the House of Commons Agriculture Committee 'received no evidence' of the horrific cruelty inherent in the intensive broiler chicken industry reflects the inadequate nature of the farm animal welfare movement's concern for broilers at that time. The broiler chicken industry operates quite literally behind closed doors, the general public seeing nothing of the birds until they appear on the supermarket shelves, at 'take-aways', on butchers' slabs or the dinner plate. Disquiet about chicken transport has been felt for decades, sparked off by the sight of lorries, as high as houses, crammed with thousands of bewildered and terrified birds, speeding towards the slaughter house. But broilers' living conditions remained a mystery to all, except poultry scientists, industry workers and the few concerned with animal welfare who made it their business to find out. However, from the mid '80s campaigns have been launched by animal welfare groups to alert the public to the cruelty behind the seemingly endless supply of cheap chicken meat, and to the health risks associated with its consumption.

CHICKEN – BRITAIN'S MOST POPULAR MEAT

Since the '60s chicken has become an increasingly cheap and popular food. By 1963, 142 million chickens were being kept intensively in the UK within the broiler system[1], that figure rising steadily to over 600 million by 1988.[2] The reason for the massive increase in chicken production is threefold.

First, poultry scientists have been able to speed up the growth of the birds dramatically, by selective breeding and the development of growth-promoting antibiotics. Today's broiler chicken weighs twice the amount at seven weeks of age as did his or her counterpart twenty five years ago.[3] Not satisfied with this achievement – which, in welfare terms, spells disaster, for reasons explained later in this chapter – poultry scientists are persisting in their research to fatten up birds even more quickly.

Secondly, intensive 'factory farming' methods have enabled farmers to keep huge numbers of birds with a minimum of labour costs. 150,000 birds or more can be attended to by one stock keeper, and in the UK over 600 million birds are reared annually on little over one thousand farms.

Thirdly, the health scares associated with fatty red meats have boosted sales of 'healthy' white chicken meat to an all-time high, encouraging existing broiler 'growers' (as intensive chicken farmers are revealingly termed) to expand, and huge companies such as Unigate have moved into a seemingly buoyant market. The cost to the consumer is attractively low, but what of the cost to the chicken?

Most chickens are supplied by specialist hatcheries which

deliver them to farms at the day-old stage, though large companies may breed, hatch and rear on the same site. At first, broiler house conditions might seem acceptable. The litter (usually woodshavings) is clean, sweet-smelling and dry, the house extremely warm, and the tiny creatures fluffy and delightful in appearance – true Easter chicks. But already they are victims of the massive nature of the system. Broiler houses, which are huge windowless sheds, vary greatly in size, each one holding anything from 5,000 to 100,000 birds, and individual attention even at this stage is impossible. Inevitably, some chicks die, disappearing into the still friable litter to decompose there. Birds which in their natural state would be kept warm under an attentive mother hen's wings, shown what to eat and generally protected by her, are exposed to a vast and stressful world. There is no respite from the birds' 'days', for the lighting is always on, except for one half hour out of every twenty four, when all lights are switched off. This is to simulate the power cut which could, in birds totally unused to darkness, cause panic and mass suffocation. Obviously, the birds sleep periodically ('like babies' as one MAFF official told me) but basically they got on with the job of eating and putting on weight, this being the sole reason for their existence. At first, lighting is bright, to enable chicks to find the food and water points, but by the third week it will have been turned down to between two and five lux, to reduce the incidence of aggression, which could lead to heart attacks. (Two to five lux is extremely dim – a helpful Electricity Board official, when trying to give an impression of its quality, likened it to moonlight.)

STOCKING DENSITY AND LITTER CONDITIONS

The accepted stocking density within the industry is 0.55 of a square foot per bird of floor space – an area considerably smaller than the cover of the Phone Book and expressed as 34kg per square metre (measured in mass body weight rather than the individual bird) in MAFF's 1987 Codes of Recommendations for the Welfare of Domestic Fowls. As the birds grow (in just seven weeks they multiply their hatched weight approximately sixty times) conditions deteriorate, until eventually the shed floor is a near-solid mass of birds, who stumble over each other in their never-ending quest to reach food and water.

Even in the best run units the litter is never changed (though if it gets wet and solid, fresh shavings may be added) and the birds' faeces contaminate it to such an extent that by the end of the growing cycle (usually seven weeks, a pathetically short 'lifespan' for birds which under natural conditions could live for as many years) 80% of what is on the floor is composed of chicken droppings. Ideally, the litter should remain friable, but frequently it becomes 'capped' by a greasy layer, rendering it useless as bedding. Imperfect ventilation, drinkers which spill over or an attack of diarrhoea in the flock can render the so-called litter nothing better than a layer of filth, from which the birds have no escape. Other causes of capped litter are the practice of feeding back blood, offal and feathers of slaughtered birds and inappropriate levels of fats and oils in the diet.

A SHORT AND DISEASED LIFE

While most broilers are slaughtered at seven weeks of age, 'Spring Chickens' or 'Poussins' are killed at around twenty-eight days, when they have just replaced their chicks' down with the first brand-new feathers, while some birds are 'grown on' to supply the market for heavier birds, particularly at Christmas time. At seven weeks broilers weigh on average five pounds (unprocessed), their staggering size contrasting grotesquely with baby-blue eyes and high-pitched vocalisation. Sexual maturity is still some twelve weeks away.

Today's poultry industry has produced a 'super' bird which in just 49 days grows to be massively too heavy for its own good. Millions of broilers suffer from painful leg and feet deformities.

Chronic respiratory disease, heart attacks (known as acute death syndrome), fatty liver/kidney syndrome, colisepticaemia and Marek's disease (a type of cancer) are just a few of the diseases which take their toll, with mortality running at around 6% – some 36 million birds succumbing each year to fatal diseases *before they reach the age of seven weeks*. G. S. Coutts BVMS MRCVS writes in *Poultry Diseases Under Modern Management*: 'A typical example of a disease, the incidence of which has increased dramatically with increasing intensivism in the poultry industry, is *colisepticaemia*. Almost unknown in the days when poultry was reared in small numbers under free range conditions, the disease increased in incidence to become one of the major obstacles to development of an intensive broiler industry.'[4] Though less of a scourge now than it was ten years ago, colisepticaemia is still a common cause of rejection, while its on-farm treatment involves the use of therapeutic antibiotics (as opposed to growth-promoting antibiotics which are taken from a range of antibiotics *not* used in human medicine). The dangers to human health arising from the widespread use of these drugs in intensive systems will be touched on in chapter 5. In the late '80s a new generation of viral diseases is emerging, with such infections as the so-called stunting syndrome (when chicks exhibit very poor growth rates) causing high mortality. Dehydration and emaciation are major causes of rejection, telling their own tale of stress and suffering.

The salmonella organism, reckoned by Dr Bernard Rowe of the Central Public Health Laboratory to be present in a high percentage of broilers by the time they are processed, may not make the birds ill, but can kill consumers of infected meat should it be handled with less than clinical care. Much poultry feed contains protein of animal origin (sometimes from already infected birds – a really vicious circle) and the bug thrives in the unhygienic conditions in intensive farms and processing plants.

Birds suffer much misery from conditions which do not necessarily kill, nor even make rejection necessary at the processing stage, so consumers run the very real risk of eating birds which have endured much pain and distress. Because of their obesity and the fact that there is little incentive or space for movement, the heavy birds spend much of their time, especially during the two or three weeks prior to slaughter, squatting down. In this position their feet, hocks (the top joint of the leg) and breasts exert great pressure on the often filthy, ammonia-ridden litter. Trevor Bray of MAFF's Agricultural Development and Advisory Service (ADAS) put it succinctly when he wrote: 'A bed-ridden human being sometimes gets bed sores. So does a broiler. Indeed one could argue that the modern docile broiler is encouraged to take a relaxed attitude to life. The trouble is that while it is sitting around, it exerts pressure on two areas of its anatomy, the hocks and the breast. If the bed on which it sits is hard and wet, downgrading may occur.'[5] Hock burns can often be detected on chickens on sale in supermarkets, though following pressure from welfare groups, the more 'upmarket' stores are attempting to overcome the problem by refusing to accept marked birds from their suppliers. A disturbing fact is that ulcerated feet are almost certainly present when hocks show severe burns. Few consumers ever see this part of the bird's anatomy, except in some small slaughter houses selling 'long legged' (i.e. complete with feet) birds to the public where large numbers may be seen with ulcers eating deep into the flesh.

When ammonia fumes are strong (the result of poor ventilation combined with dirty litter) keratoconjunctivitis can render birds blind, and this condition is especially painful; affected birds attempt to rub their smarting eyes with their wings, and let out cries of pain. Perosis, a very common disease among broilers (caused by dietary deficiencies) involves enlargement of the hock joint, resulting in crippling and severe pain, but unless the affected bird is found to be emaciated, or showing signs of secondary infection, the carcase will not be rejected. The chicken legs which form the centrepiece for many a buffet party may well have born a weight of suffering!

TO THE SLAUGHTERHOUSE

Perhaps the worst stress of all in broilers' short lives comes at the time of catching when, usually in the dead of night, gangs of catchers move in to clear the houses. Birds are grabbed by their legs and carried upside down, several in each catcher's hands, to be thrust into crates and loaded on to lorries. Hips are frequently dislocated and many other injuries sustained, including bruising (a very common cause for rejection) and broken wings and legs. As with battery hens, processors reckon on a percentage of birds being dead on arrival – the figure of ½% – 1% was given at one major plant, which nationwide would account for up to six million birds each year. The length of journey, prevailing weather conditions and (probably the most significant factor) time spent on the lorry waiting for unloading all affect the DOA figures.

'Downgrading' – that is injury to birds which decreases their market value – is a headache for the industry. Since welfarists have been putting pressure on retailers about hock burns (sometimes called 'black hocks') processors are in turn putting pressure on producers to reduce visible damage to birds: 'Maurice Race is back in broilers after a twenty five year gap to find that packers are "black hock" crazy. He is allowed 5%, but anything above that and the price falls by 2p a lb'.[6] With growers selling at below production costs at the time of writing (already the bubble has burst), this penalty is a stiff one.

Cliff Stuart, a veterinarian writing in *Poultry World* in February 1985, lists some of the reasons for downgrading in broilers: 'Poor environmental conditions on the farm, including overcrowding, poor ventilation and diet induced scouring (salt/fats) and inadequately managed drinking systems, causing wet litter, influence the incidence of breast blisters, ammonia burns on the breast, burnt hocks and leg problems. Any disease which makes a bird disinclined to walk will increase the numbers of breast blisters . . . Green discoloured bruises and septic lesions are obviously due to on-farm damage and will be increased in flighty flocks, those flocks which have been continually upset. Old back scratches due to overcrowding or panic show up as scar tissue or septic areas . . . Bruising is one of the major causes of downgrading. Variation from company to company can often be associated with the speed of catching, the transport system used, quality and general attitude of the staff, and, last but not least, the degree and quality of supervisors.'

Consumers should remember that 'downgrading' often applies only to the visual aspect of slaughtered birds, and birds deemed at least in part fit for human consumption may have suffered from the raw wounds of ulcers, ammonia blindness and many other painful conditions. Chicken pieces, or portions, are often the salvaged parts of injured birds – severe bruising or breast blisters may condemn one part of the chicken to the processed or pet food trade, while the legs, for example, even if broken, will be packaged up for the supermarket.

The slaughter of broilers has been investigated with disturbing findings. G B S Heath, FRCVS, a (now retired) Official Veterinary Surgeon (OVS) previously employed by the South Northants District Council under the Poultry Meat (Hygiene) Regulations, wrote in 1984: 'The consensus is that about one third of all broilers are not stunned, so this means that, every day in the UK, more than half a million are sentient when they go to the knife.'[7] Worse still, Mr Heath's research indicated that some birds enter the scalding tank fully conscious. Happily, due to Mr Heath's revelations and pressure from welfarists, steps have been taken at some, but by no means all, processing plants to use the 'stun/kill' method, whereby higher voltage electric shocks ensure a far greater proportion of birds rendered unconscious until death supervenes. This development must be seen as a welcome welfare improvement, but the terrors of catching, transport (when birds may travel hundreds of miles, to wait for hours in freezing or sweltering conditions outside the processing plant) and slaughter itself can scarcely be exaggerated.

Another improvement is the broiler 'harvester', a machine which enables birds to be scooped up by rubber paddles, thus avoiding manhandling at any stage. This automated system may sound chillingly 'brave new world' but certainly represents a great improvement in welfare terms on the old crude method of catching. However, the harvester is only in its infancy. The design of many broiler houses does not lend itself to its introduction, nor does the device do anything more than significantly *reduce* stress and injuries among the terrified birds (heartbeats of 'harvested' birds return to normal more quickly than do those of birds caught manually).[8]

After the broiler sheds are cleared out, most lie empty for three weeks to allow for the removal of old litter, cleansing and fumigating, and preparing the house for the next batch of chicks. Most 'growers' put through five crops of chickens each year (the arable terminology sticks in my throat, but I will use it for convenience) though some fit in six. When the sheds are empty, it is an eerie sight indeed, the only reminder of the thousands of young lives being a layer of filthy litter and often the remains of those victims of the system that died at various ages, and whose bodies escaped the notice of the stock keeper. Frequently, decomposing carcases may be seen in litter from broiler houses, spread as fertilizer on farmland.

THE BREEDING STOCK

But what of the parent stock, which provides the millions of eggs from which broiler chickens are hatched? According to MAFF figures, over six million birds fulfilled this role in 1987. These birds, generally at a ratio of ten hens to one cockerel, are kept for around sixty four weeks, after which their peak time of production is over and they are slaughtered for roasting or to be used in pies etc. Adult birds weigh on average 9 lbs, except for the estimated 2.5% of 'Mini-mums', hens specially bred to be only half the usual size, yet who produce normal sized chicks. The attraction to breeders of mini-mums is that they eat much less and take up less room, but they require a higher degree of stockmanship, being easily upset and put off lay, so their popularity is limited. Almost all parent stock are kept on deep litter, though at least one UK flock is caged. (Caged hens are artificially inseminated.) Some females are debeaked, but the cockerels never are, since they must be able to grasp the females necks firmly when mating.

Figures for mortality and culls are high among broiler breeders, being 38% for males and 6% for females over the first 24 weeks, the higher incidence of culled males reflecting the stringent selection for the best breeders. Culled birds are sold for human consumption. From 25 weeks of age till slaughter, mortality runs at 15% for males and 6% for females. The most common diseases suffered by parent stock are reproductive disorders (no doubt resulting from the intolerable strain put on the birds by selective breeding for reproductive prowess), various viral conditions, including viral tenosynovitis (an extremely painful condition), leukosis and Marek's disease, the last two conditions being cancerous. The leukosis complex of diseases is caused by a tumour producing virus, and though it 'can be very common in broilers, especially lymphoid leukosis'[9] may not always show itself when birds are young and being slaughtered for human consumption. It could however be latent, since the condition is often passed through the egg, only becoming a full-blown disease *in birds allowed to attain maturity*. A rare member of the leukosis 'family' is osteopetrosis, described as a zoonotic disease (i.e. transferable to humans) by R. N. Kay BSc MRCVS, author of *Poultry Meat Inspectors' Training Manual*, published by Derbyshire Dales District Council. Mr Kay stresses the absolute necessity of rejecting any birds with leukosis.

Injuries to broiler parent stock may be due to mating by heavy birds and dislocations caused by activities such as jumping down from a small height which in non-obese birds would cause no damage.

Because broilers have been bred to eat well and put on weight rapidly they are, not surprisingly, 'greedy' as a result. Consequently, it is usual in the broiler industry to restrict the more long-lived broiler breeders' rations, except during the few weeks either side of the onset of lay. The practice of breeding creatures whose main aims and pleasures revolve around eating, then deliberately restricting their food, is yet another indication of the inhumane nature of the system. An ugly picture of deprivation is drawn perhaps unwittingly by the veterinarian G. S. Coutts when he writes about the causes of staphylococcal arthritis in poultry: 'The condition is caused by Staphylococcus aureus which invades the tissues or blood stream, following injury to the skin, especially the feet. The infection then tends to localise in the joints, tendons and adjacent tissues. Any environmental factor which may result in skin injury; e.g. sharp projections, wood splinters in litter, or birds suffering injury when rushing to the feeders where feed restriction is practised (in broiler breeders particularly) will result in an increased incidence of the condition'.[10]

Salmonella, campylobacter and listeria are now words with ugly and frightening connotations for consumers. It is no coincidence that they are all strongly associated with the intensive poultry industry, which for too long has imposed its regime of ruthless exploitation on billions of defenceless victims.

Chapter 3
Intensive Egg and Chicken Production and the Law

> 'The authorities should be ready to prosecute not only in cases of wilful or persistent disregard of the law, but also cases of neglect or carelessness in which exemplary consequences would have a useful deterrent effect. They should also seek occasion to bring some test cases to determine the adequacy of the 1968 Act. Inspection and enforcement should remain with the State Veterinary Service, who should co-operate fully with voluntary bodies.' (Page 51, 'Summary of Conclusions and Recommendations', House of Commons First Report from the Agriculture Committee, session 1980–81.)

The massive battery egg and broiler chicken industries have evolved in an arbitrary fashion as far as the law of the land is concerned, allowing a bizarre situation to develop. Farmers all over the United Kingdom are operating systems which are, in essence, illegal, and recent additions to legislation (designed to apply specifically to intensively-kept farm animals) have merely served to highlight the impossibility of protecting poultry kept within systems which carry intensivism to extremes.

The Protection of Animals Act, 1911 forbids any person to 'cause any unnecessary suffering, or, being the owner, permit any unnecessary suffering to be caused to any animal...'. The Agriculture (Miscellaneous Provisions) Act 1968 being 'an Act to make further provisions with respect to the welfare of livestock' states, under the subheading 'Prevention of unnecessary pain and distress for livestock': 'Any person who causes unnecessary pain or unnecessary distress to any livestock for the time being situated on agricultural land and under his control or permits any such livestock to suffer any such pain or distress of which he knows or may reasonably be expected to know shall be guilty of an offence under this section.' Two very important additions to the 1968 Act will be discussed later in this chapter.

CAN SUFFERING BE 'NECESSARY'?

One school of thought suggests that the suffering of farm animals kept in widely adopted systems may be deemed 'necessary' in a court of law, since food production could not be envisaged on a comparable scale under any other system. Alternative systems do already exist for egg and chicken production but at the time of writing they could not supply consumers' demands, since the free range market accounts for only around 5% of egg production and a small proportion of 1% of chickens. This viewpoint may have some foundation in strictly legal terms, but should a society which assumes itself to be civilised accept such a judgement?

Leaving aside the cruel concept of necessary suffering, let us consider the implications of the 1911 and 1968 Acts (which on the surface seem well formulated for the purpose of protecting animals and ensuring their welfare) and see how these Acts are used, and by whom.

On 21 January 1987 the Minister of Agriculture's Private Secretary wrote: 'Members of the State Veterinary Service do in fact carry out a programme of visits to farms to ensure that the provisions of the codes are met and to advise stock keepers on any necessary action in order to improve the conditions under which their birds are kept. When such advice is persistently or flagrantly ignored, we take action through the courts to ensure that such perpetrators are brought to book.'[1] Fighting words, but how do they square with the facts?

On 28 April 1988 Andrew Smith, MP, put the following Parliamentary Question: 'To ask the Minister of Agriculture, Fisheries and Food, what was the number of: a) prosecutions and b) convictions in respect of unnecessary pain or distress caused to broiler and battery chickens in each of the last five years.' Donald Thompson, Parliamentary Secretary, replied that three successful prosecutions had been taken, one each in '87, '86 and '83. Not a great number, you may think, considering that collectively some 2,500 million broilers and battery hens went through the system during this five year period. Yet anyone with knowledge of MAFF's track record on prosecutions might be forgiven for harbouring suspicions that Mr Thompson was indulging in exaggeration. Being one such person, I embarked on an enquiry which was to take several weeks of letters and telephone calls to Whitehall and MAFF's Animal Health Department at Tolworth in Surrey. Finally I elicited this statement from Henry Brown of MAFF's Animal Welfare Division: 'I am sorry this has taken such a long time to deal with, but we have had to delve back in our files to check the details. This exercise has revealed that the reply given to Mr Andrew Smith MP on 28 April was not quite correct. The three prosecutions mentioned did take place, and did lead to convictions, but the Ministry prosecuted only in the 1986 case.'[2] Add to this the following statement from MAFF: 'Thank you for your letter of 12 August 1985 to Mrs Peggy Fenner about Court action taken by this Ministry against producers for causing unnecessary pain or unnecessary distress to poultry. The Ministry has not found it necessary to take any such action against a poultry producer in the last ten years'[3] and the picture of MAFF's torpidity in this area is complete.

THE ROTHERHAM CASE: STILL AN EXCEPTION

The one and only MAFF prosecution in the last fifteen years, the 1987 one (incorrectly dated by MAFF – in fact the trial was adjourned several times during the period May '86 to March '87), involved M. B. Burgess Ltd, a farm/slaughterhouse specialising in ritual slaughter, and sometimes patronised by MAFF when turning out birds from its experimental husbandry farm at Gleadthorpe. The case was heard at Rotherham Magistrates' Court and resulted from a MAFF inspection which revealed severe neglect of a flock of broiler chickens being 'grown on' for the Christmas trade in larger birds. A MAFF vet from Leeds had found the four week old birds to be affected by pododermatitis (ulcers on the soft undersides of the feet) due to standing on filthy litter. Unfortunately, the vet did not return in a week or two to check on conditions, but, inexplicably, made his next visit *ten weeks later*, by which time the same birds were living on litter which was subsequently described by MAFF's prosecuting solicitor as 'wet and soggy'. Birds were now found to be suffering from very severe foot ulceration, with severe hock burns and breast blisters. Five carcases were removed and taken to the (now closed) Leeds Veterinary Investigation Centre. Examination there revealed a tumour of the ovary in one bird which had spread throughout the body cavity, and in other birds tenosynivitis (a painful condition when 'birds will be found sitting on their hocks, having great difficulty in walking'),[4] pressure lesions on foot pads and hocks, empty stomachs and numerous counts of bacteria in hock burns. Previously, Burgess' own vet had found Marek's disease to be present in the flock.

It emerged at the trial that over the twelve month period June '85 – June '86 (the broilers which were the subject of the prosecution lived and died during this time) 896,000 chickens passed through the Kiveton slaughter plant owned by M B Burgess Ltd. Of these, only 0.3% were condemned as being unfit for human consumption. With abysmally low husbandry standards and diseases including cancer identified on at least one farm supplying the plant these figures are disturbing in the extreme. This isolated example of MAFF showing its teeth ended with the culprit being fined £600.

But why was not the Rotherham case just one among dozens – hundreds even – of similar cases, since the conditions exposed during the hearing are by no means unusual? The state of broilers bought by Chickens' Lib from various sources has indicated that on many farms feet ulceration and hock burns are the rule rather than the exception, and severe foot and leg deformities abound in these heavy birds. The Official Veterinary Surgeon (OVSs are appointed by MAFF) at a leading poultry processing plant has informed me that tenosynivitis, emaciation and dehydration top the list of reasons for rejection of poultry meat – these conditions being connected, since birds with tenosynivitis find difficulty in walking, so cannot reach food and water points.

Why does MAFF fail to take action when it is known that many procedures and conditions on factory farms cause suffering? For example, feed restriction in broiler breeders can, as we have seen, indirectly trigger off Staphylococcus aureus infections and the sheer size of broiler houses ensures ongoing welfare problems. Repeated complaints to MAFF about conditions on *named* farms, or about birds bought from markets or slaughterhouses *whose farms of origin could be traced* have failed to result in legal proceedings by MAFF, despite the obvious fact, emphasised in the Agriculture Committee's Summary quoted at the beginning of this chapter, that prosecutions 'would have a useful deterrent effect'. It was hoped by many concerned with animal welfare that the Rotherham case would set a precedent. M. B. Burgess Ltd was accused by MAFF of causing birds 'a great deal of pain' and 'extreme pain', but what of the farmers who routinely turn out birds with hock burns, often so teeming with bacteria that the outer scabs must be scraped off at the processing stage to enable the chickens to be passed fit for human consumption, and with ulcers eating deep into the soft pads of the feet?

MAFF takes a gloomy view of its chances of success in the courts. 'In the first place MAFF would not take a prosecution unless it believed, in all the circumstances of the case, that there was a very good chance of obtaining a conviction. One of the main circumstances that would have to be taken into account in deciding whether to prosecute in a broiler case is the incidence of the problem among the flock. For example, it could obviously be very difficult to secure a conviction if only a small proportion of the birds were affected among a flock of several thousand.'[5] Leaving aside the point that the animal protection laws are intended to protect *the individual bird*, this statement sounds like an excuse for doing nothing. Furthermore, Chickens' Lib has reported instances of hundreds of birds piled high in slaughterhouses when it could be seen at a glance that whole flocks had been suffering from ugly foot ulceration, yet MAFF has refused to prosecute.

In May 1985, Ron Pugh, a MAFF poultry advisor, explained in the pages of *Poultry World*: 'Damp or greasy litter caused burnt hocks, and, to an extent, recent industry concern over the problem has been retailer-led. Because hocks were prominent in the way the whole birds were presented in the UK, even a burn spot was enough to cause down-grading. *In winter reared flocks, down-grading could reach 100%*' (My italics.) No mention of the ulcerated feet which often accompany hock burns – these signs of 'unnecessary pain and unnecessary distress' are no one's worry, being chopped off at the processing stage, to be tossed into evil-smelling bins and sold to manufacturers of pet food or fertilizers.

Since the potential for suffering within the battery cage has been widely recognised for many years, it is especially shocking that battery farmers who offend under the 1911 and 1968 Acts have been treated with such remarkable tolerance by MAFF. Battery hens suffer life-long imprisonment, and as we have seen the cage system promotes cage layer fatigue, brittle bones, egg laying problems and extreme and prolonged stress. Tumours, the cause of death (or rejection at processing plants) in many battery hens, are unlikely to be detected in the cage situation, and it is routine practice for 'deads' to be removed on a daily basis – though death often comes as the final stage of a period of prolonged ill-health and suffering. Animal welfarists have often drawn MAFF's attention to horrifying conditions within specific units, yet no prosecutions have ensued. It has been left to the RSPCA, a charity with no right of entry to farms, or to local authorities, to take action. Between 1973 and 1988 the RSPCA has been successful in obtaining 505 'cruelty to fowl' convictions.

On January 1st 1979 the Welfare of Livestock (Intensive Units) Regulations came into force, since when 'a person who fails to comply with the provisions of the preceding regulations shall be guilty of an offence under section 2 of the Agriculture (Miscellaneous Provisions) Act 1968'.[6] These regulations were drawn up with the avowed intention of protecting the welfare of animals kept within farming systems reliant on automatic equipment 'to such an extent that failure of that equipment will cause the livestock to suffer unnecessary pain or unnecessary distress unless the failure is rectified or other provision is made for the care of the livestock.' For battery hens, this piece of legislation has already been superseded by the 1987 Welfare of Battery Hens Regulations, so we will first look at the 1987 Regulations vis à vis broilers, to which they still apply.

The regulations are short and to the point. Any failure of equipment must be 'rectified forthwith' or provision made to safeguard the livestock from any unnecessary pain or unnecessary distress (known as UPUD in MAFF circles). The regulations also state – and here the lawmakers fell into a trap which should have been apparent – that 'the livestock shall be thoroughly inspected by a keeper not less than once a day to check that it is in a state of well-being'. Apparently MAFF regards the exercise of inspecting vast numbers of dimly-lit, loose-housed birds as a feasible one – but the real world of factory farming is far removed from the neat pages of the statute book, or the desk tops of Whitehall. Broiler farms being erected at the time of writing by Unigate, as part of its massive grant-aided development in Humberside, consist of ten sheds per site, each destined to contain 35,000 birds, with two stock keepers responsible for the welfare of the sum total of 350,000. Some broiler farmers keep flocks of up to 100,000 birds under one roof. A Somerset farmer with 88,000 birds together in one shed, boasted in *Poultry World* (5 December 1985) of extra time spent in bed because of an efficient new system of feeders and drinkers: 'I used to get up in the small hours of the morning to prepare for the catchers – now I wait until I hear the lorries coming down the lane . . .' The article goes on: 'When you do the work yourself and also farm sixty acres without employees, that's important.' MAFF, when preparing new legislation, should have been aware of the present unacceptable conditions in the broiler industry, and the absolute impossibility of inspecting broiler chickens 'thoroughly'.

As mentioned in an earlier chapter, in the vast sheds tiny chicks die and disappear in the litter, and birds of all ages can frequently be seen at various stages of decomposition when the time comes for used litter to be spread on fields as fertiliser. These trampled remains are proof that birds sicken and die unheeded and in large numbers in the dimly-lit sheds where 'healthy' chicken meat is produced. Consumers of beef may not be pleased to know that MAFF recommends feeding minimally treated broiler litter, and all it might contain, to beef cattle despite the fact that they 'do not much like the taste of chicken litter, and ADAS (MAFF's Agricultural Development and Advisory Service) advises that it should be introduced into their diets gradually.'[7] In a recent outbreak of botulism among 150 housed beef cattle sixty eight of the animals died. Decomposing poultry carcases in the litter incorporated into their feed were found to be the source of infection. ('A major outbreak of botulism in cattle being fed ensiled poultry litter' – *Veterinary Record*, 11 June 1988.)

IS THE SYSTEM ITSELF ILLEGAL?

Mortality aside, millions of birds suffer from painful conditions which go undetected *because of the very nature of intensive systems*. Professor Ekesbo of the Swedish University of Agricultural Sciences at Skara wrote about intensive farming systems in *Veterinary Practice* (3 July 1987): 'If a daily health control cannot be easily and correctly made, disease conditions may worsen before discovery, which causes unnecessary suffering for the animals. The reason for the design of such animal housing may be the widespread assumption or delusion that health can be controlled only by a daily control of the production figures, without looking at the animals.'

If MAFF's view that only a small proportion of some flocks (among many thousands of birds, this 'small proportion' could run into hundreds or thousands of broiler chickens) may be affected by hock burns or foot ulcers, the logical conclusion must surely be that vast numbers of birds should be individually inspected to ensure finding the ailing birds. In humane husbandry systems this would scarcely be necessary, since the type of health hazards run by factory-farmed broilers would be unlikely to threaten the birds, individually or as a flock. On factory farms thorough inspection is necessary, but impossible to achieve.

Sick birds may fail to reach food and water points so emaciation and dehydration are, as we have seen, very common causes for rejection at processing plants. MAFF's Broiler Production Wall Chart (revised in 1985) recommends that when chicks are four or five days old brooder lights should be switched off, and 'if Tungsten bulbs, dim gradually from 50–100 lux to reach 2–5 lux by day fifteen.' Dim indeed, for MAFF in its leaflet 185 *Roaster/Heavy Chicken Production* warns: 'Operators should provide a minimum of 2 lux light intensity for the main rearing period with from 10–20 lux for the first 1–2 days in order to accustom the birds to the location of food and water.' Thus are birds, known for their sharp eyesight, relegated to extreme gloom for most of their short lives. In the same leaflet MAFF does by implication, though not of course by intention, condemn the broiler system as illegal: 'Heavy table chickens are subject to all the normal disease hazards of litter-housed birds. In addition, the problem of leg disorders which is experienced with conventional broiler growing is accentuated when birds are retained to a greater age ... However ... if birds become lame they can often be killed and processed before deterioration leads to a second quality carcase. Thus a thorough daily stock inspection is doubly important, *although it is realised that identifying the early stages of leg disorders among large flocks can be difficult.*' (My italics.)

The catalogue of diseases which are both caused and hidden by the system is endless. No one has yet been able to give a satisfactory explanation of how a stock keeper can 'thoroughly' inspect many thousands of birds, as is required by law. At best, conditions which could lead to severe economic loss can be noted, such as respiratory distress or an outbreak of diarrhoea. But painful and distressing conditions like perosis, when hock joints become twisted, go unnoticed in the dimly-lit mass of moving bodies.

On 1 January 1988 the Welfare of Battery Hens Regulations 1987 came into force, implementing the EEC Council Directive 86/113/EEC and stipulating, for the first time, legal requirements throughout the EEC on space allowance for caged hens. These regulations require a minimum floor area of 450 sq cm by 1995 for all cages, while cages built or put into use for the first time on or after 1 January 1988 must afford birds the minimum floor space from this earlier date.

Point 8 in the Regulations' Schedule states: 'The flock or group of laying hens shall be thoroughly inspected at least once a day and for this purpose a source of light shall be available which is strong enough for each bird to be seen clearly, and, if need be, thoroughly inspected.' The subtle change in wording from the 1978 Regulations: 'The livestock shall be thoroughly inspected by a stock keeper not less than once a day to check that it is in a state of well-being' to the more convoluted requirement of the 1987 Regulations leads one to wonder at the motivation behind the change, yet does not appear to substantially alter the meaning of the Regulations. If the stock keeper must see enough to decide whether he or she needs to see more, then they will need to have a fairly good look at each individual bird in the first place. In the gloom and stench of a battery house this is asking a lot of the most dedicated stock keeper! The dry heat and dust in battery houses, often combined with high levels of ammonia in the air, discourage workers from carrying out duties beyond those which are obviously vital. People susceptible to bronchitis are made worse by battery house conditions. The National Union of Agricultural and Allied Workers, in a written answer to the 1980–81 House of Commons enquiry into poultry, pig and veal production stated: 'As to workers' personal preference, the view seems to be that they would prefer to work out of doors, and that is often why they choose to work in agriculture . . . Poultry workers have expressed dissatisfaction with the heat and dust that appear always to be present in intensive poultry houses.'[8]

RSPCA PROSECUTES A BATTERY FARMER

A brave attempt was made by the RSPCA in 1981 to exploit the obvious loophole in the 1978 Regulations when the Society brought a successful prosecution against a Surrey battery farmer on the grounds that he failed to 'thoroughly' inspect his flocks of birds, which consisted of around 6,000 chicks in one shed and approximately 7,000 layers in two other buildings. Members of the Society's Special Investigations Unit (as it was then called) lay in wait over a 24 hour period, establishing that the farmer spent a total of 9.5 minutes in the sheds, while two boys aged 15 and 16 took just under 3 hours to collect eggs (they did not enter the chicks' shed), placing egg trays in front of any cages holding dead birds. Clearly, the dead birds were left in close proximity to their fellow cage mates whose job it still was to lay 'farm fresh' eggs, until sometime during the following day.

The RSPCA used daring tactics to obtain the necessary evidence. One of the officers trespassed three times during the course of their watch, first to place gravel on padlocks on any doors out of sight at the far end of the sheds, and then to check whether it had been disturbed. In the event, the farmer was fined £150 with £250 costs, and despite the meagre nature of the fine it looked as if the typically lawless behaviour of intensive poultry keepers had been exposed. A clear indication that this Surrey farmer's behaviour *was* typical was given when Derek Crane, a MAFF poultry adviser, pinpointed the following causes of feed waste among battery hens: 'Overfeeding of stock, running hoppers too often, *'feeding up' on Fridays to avoid weekend feeding.*' (My italics)[9] The likelihood that many millions of intensively-housed birds are neglected at weekends and on public holidays is great, and perhaps it is no coincidence that mass deaths among poultry from suffocation following breakdowns in electrical and ventilation systems have occurred on Bank Holiday weekends. During the 1987 August Bank Holiday, 70,000 battery hens owned by the New Dawn Group (a cruel misnomer) suffocated following a power failure.

At the time of the RSPCA prosecution the editor of *Poultry World*, himself a battery farmer, wrote revealingly: 'To make this point about inspection of poultry in intensive units RSPCA men have suffered considerable discomfort, trespassed on a Surrey farmer's land and made the whole process of looking after the well-being of stock utterly ridiculous. There can be few better examples of the law being an ass through man's attempts to define legislation that is beyond him . . . Still I am wondering what (the farmer) did wrong in a mass management system that depends on catering for flocks not individual birds. Quite rightly he was concerned about flock health and maintaining the best environment for the flock. When we fail to do that we deserve all the RSPCA can throw at us, but not for failing to look every bird in the eye every day.'[10]

Though intensive poultry farmers would like to interpret the law as referring to flocks rather than to individual birds, the Dorking case successfully established that the individual bird is protected by the 1978 Regulations, and it was stated by a vet acting for the RSPCA that birds *would have to be removed from their cages* in order for a truly 'thorough' inspection to be made. The NFU supported Mr Constable (the farmer in question) throughout the case; one may draw one's own conclusions from its eventual decision not to appeal. Inexplicably, the RSPCA took no further cases of this nature, and Mr Constable finished up a lone scapegoat. Had case after case followed, as surely should have happened, the course of factory farming in this country could have been dramatically altered.

MAFF WELFARE CODES

MAFF issues welfare codes. Leaflet 703 applies to domestic fowls and was revised in 1987. Optimistically, the 'Introduction by Ministers' states: 'Welfare Codes are intended to encourage stock keepers to adopt the highest standards of husbandry . . . The Code itself, which has the approval of Parliament, embodies the latest scientific advice and the best current husbandry practices and takes into account the five basic needs: freedom from thirst, hunger and malnutrition; appropriate comfort and shelter; the prevention, or rapid diagnosis and treatment of, injury, disease or infestation; freedom from fear; and freedom to display most normal patterns of behaviour.'

In reality, the Code embodies an amazing number of examples of illogicality, self-contradiction and confusion. Can the Ministers be serious? Can the Code purport to apply to broilers crouching shoulder to shoulder on solid stinking litter, often dying of malnutrition and dehydration, forced to defecate over each other and dragging themselves on weak and often deformed limbs through the intense gloom to the nearest food and water points? Can the Code be intended to have any application to the welfare of battery hens as they spend up to two years unable to turn round without jostling one another, forever denied the chance to spread their wings, living out their lives of never-ending stress and deprivation?

Something a little nearer reality emerges under the heading 'Housing', in paragraph 13, where it is admitted, in a burst of uncharacteristic candour: 'The design and usage of some battery cages of the kind at present in use for laying hens places severe restrictions on the birds' freedom to turn round without difficulty, groom themselves, get up and sit down, rest undisturbed, stretch their legs and body and perform wing-flapping and dust-bathing behaviour as well as to fulfil other health and welfare needs. Cages should be designed and maintained so as to minimise discomfort and distress and to prevent injury to the birds being caused by such restrictions.'

MAFF has issued Codes, approved by the British Parliament, which itemise the 'severe restrictions' imposed by the battery cage system in language which would hardly disgrace an animal rights pressure group! One could be forgiven for interpreting paragraph 13 as an indictment of the battery hen system, and an indication of its illegal nature. Presumably the Codes' Jekyll-and-Hyde nature reflects the pressure from animal welfarists, including those who serve on MAFF's own Farm Animal Welfare Council, and perhaps some within the ministry itself.

THE EUROPEAN CONVENTION

In January 1979 Britain followed the example of several European countries and ratified the European Convention for the Protection of Animals Kept for Farming Purposes. It did this regardless of the fact that no country should ratify a convention the requirements of which cannot be met under existing circumstances and legislation. Article 3 of this convention states: 'Animals shall be housed and provided with food, water and care in a manner which – having regard to their species and to their degree of development, adaptation and domestication – is appropriate to their physiological and ethological needs in accordance with established experience and scientific knowledge.' While article 4 is surely unambiguous to the ordinary citizen: '1) The freedom of movement appropriate to an animal, having regard to its species and in accordance with established experience and scientific knowledge, shall not be restricted in such a manner as to cause it unnecessary suffering or injury. 2) Where an animal is continuously or regularly tethered or confined, it shall be given the space appropriate to its physiological and ethological needs in accordance with established experience and scientific knowledge.'

The phrase 'in accordance with established and scientific knowledge' could constitute a 'let-out' clause, but how convincing would such a ploy be, if indeed evasiveness were the intention of those officials responsible for drawing up this convention? Are 'established experience' and 'scientific knowledge' about animals kept for farming purposes so much in their infancy that poultry specialists can plead ignorance of the sufferings of factory-farmed birds?

In 1980 the Society of Veterinary Ethology (an international scientific body founded in 1967 in response to a request from the Brambell Committee for more information on the behavioural needs of farm animals) presented a paper entitled 'Information on Behaviour and Diseases of the Laying Hen' to the Standing Committee of this same European convention. The paper indicated that poultry scientists have *for many years* been aware of the inability of battery cages to meet the physiological and ethological needs of the laying hen. Here are a few examples of research findings based on 'established experience and scientific knowledge'. Please note the dates of the research papers, which reach back to the early sixties. (Some of the language is quaint or incorrect, due to poor translation.)

- 'Among scientists studying the pre-laying behaviour of the hen it is an unanimous opinion that light hybrid hens kept in cages are frustrated in the pre-laying period. The hens show increased levels of stereotyped pacing when oviposition is near, and this can be reduced by the provision of litter. They also show increased levels of aggression at a corresponding time, and aggression is regarded as another response of frustration.' (Wood-Gush and Gilbert, 1969;

Duncan 1970; Duncan and Wood-Gush, 1971; Wood-Gush, 1972; Hughes, 1979).
- 'Dustbathing occurs as vacuum activity and in an incomplete form in cages.' (Black and Hughes, 1974; Wennrich, 1975).
- 'According to Wennrich (1975) hens allowed to leave their cages for a short time at once make bilateral wingstretching and wingflapping. In the cages these behaviour patterns were not observed.'
- 'The reduction in bilateral wingstretching and wingflapping in the cage can be explained by the physical restrictions. Accordingly Bareham (1976) found more wingflapping in an experimental cage (height approximately 45 cm). The prevention of movements especially of flying and of wingflapping reduces the strength of the wing bones and may result in broken wings.' (Somonsen and Vestergaard, 1978).
- 'Damages may be caused by the physical environment and by wear from non-pecking contact with flock mates. Lack of appropriate material for dustbathing activities may be an important factor, as it is well known that the hens perform dust bathing activity directly on the wire floor (Wennrich, 1975; Verstergaard, 1977) which lack the positive effect of dust. The forceful contact with wire floor or other environmental constructions during dust bathing activity probably has a negative effect on the plumage. Hughes and Duncan (1979) found more feather and skin damage on hens on wire floors as compared to hens on litter.'
- 'In the caged hen the environment may impose two bone diseases, namely 1) general bone weakness and 2) cage layer fatigue (CLF). From the literature it appears that bone weakness is a problem in spent layers (Rowland and Harms, 1970; Ferguson et al, 1974; Moore et al, 1977), as the condition results in broken bones accordingly in reduced carcase value.'

- 'Generally bone strength measures show that caged hens have weaker bones than deep litter hens.'
- 'Cage layer fatigue is a clinically manifest disease which may represent a final stage of the general bone weakness. The disease especially affects highly producing hens which lay eggs with normal shells. The symptoms are lameness and stop of laying. Like with general bone weakness the hens have weak bones but even more pronounced. (Bell and Siller, 1962). CLF almost exclusively occurs in cages (Bell and Siller, 1962; Riddell et al, 1968) and transfer of the hens to litter pens shows optimal curative effect (Hungerford, 1969; Riddel et al, 1968). Thus again, lack of motion seems the most significant factor. Although the second state (CLF) clinically is rarely observed the bone weakness of caged hens in general indicates that a traditional battery cage gives insufficient space for hens' normal and necessary movements.'

The above findings, which span nearly a quarter of a century, are chillingly clear. The cage system promotes suffering and disease and cannot meet the physiological or ethological needs of laying hens. (So little disquiet has been felt about the welfare of broilers, that to date little concern has been expressed by poultry research scientists.) Successive governments have ignored not only representations by ordinary people concerned with animal welfare, but the findings of those qualified to make scientific judgements. Laws have been passed, codes drawn up and a convention ratified, none of which has any relevance to conditions down on the factory farms. There, millions of battery hens and broiler chickens – and other species outside the scope of this book – continue to live out their lives in misery and squalor.

Chapter 4
The Role of the Ministry of Agriculture, Fisheries and Food (MAFF)

> 'I know of no better, cleaner system of producing eggs in the quantity we require. There's not a system better for production and for the bird itself.' Donald Thompson, MAFF's Parliamentary Secretary describing the battery system at the 1988 European Poultry Fair.

British Food and Farming Year was planned for 1989, in part to celebrate the centenary of the Ministry of Agriculture, first known as the Board of Agriculture when Lord Salisbury set it up following a crisis in agriculture prices. Since one of its present responsibilities is carrying out farm welfare inspections, with the alleged purpose of ensuring that animals are not suffering unnecessary pain or unnecessary distress, it is fair to ask the question: How is it that massive industries which promote farm animal suffering on an almost unimaginable scale have been allowed to grow and prosper over the last three or four decades? The battery hen and broiler chicken industries are prime examples of modern farm animal abuses still championed by MAFF. Far from welcoming any well-informed criticism from those concerned with animal welfare, MAFF officials are defensive in the extreme – at the 1988 European Poultry Fair Donald Thompson, MAFF's Parliamentary Secretary, warned the industry that welfare lobbies posed an increasing threat: 'These lobbies will get stronger and are getting a wider scientific basis from which to attack all aspects of *our* (my italics!) industry, and it will not be just the broiler and battery eggs systems which will be attacked, but turkeys and ducks as well.'[1]

As long ago as 1948 L. F. Easterbrook wrote in *Picture Post* about the deprivations of the battery hen, describing how their brittle bones (the result of enforced inactivity) 'snap like dry twigs'. In a civilised society compassion and common sense should ensure that animals are protected from abuse. Certainly, many children are acutely aware of the immorality of factory farming methods, as the following extracts from letters from two twelve-year-olds (a boy and a girl respectively) illustrate: 'I am pleased to write to you. In 1985 I went to the Royal Show in Stoneleigh, Warwickshire and I was enjoying myself. Till I went into a shed and there was about 300 to 400 hens in it. I felt sick and I came out and I was sick.' 'I am writing about my feelings on battery farming. I think it is very cruel and wrong that birds should be kept in small cramped cages with about four other birds, not being able to stretch their wings or wander around and see daylight. Think what life is like for those poor birds who should have comfort and freedom . . . People should have punishment for making the birds' lives so miserable and so painful.'[2] Children's views aside, there is now a vast accumulation of scientific evidence to prove conclusively that factory-farmed animals suffer, yet MAFF continues loyally to uphold the status quo. Here are a few examples of MAFF attitudes, dating from the '70s to 1988.

- 'As I have explained to you, we consider the battery cage system an acceptable method of production under proper management.' (Letter from MAFF to Chickens' Lib, 10 August 1973.)
- 'However there is no evidence that intensive husbandry systems are necessarily detrimental to animal welfare . . .' (Letter from MAFF to Chickens' Lib, 14 August 1974.)
- 'Normally it is not profitable for producers to keep bat-

tery hens after the age of 70–76 weeks when they cease to lay at an economic level, but most of the birds are in excellent bodily condition when they are sent for slaughter.' (Letter from MAFF to a Chickens' Lib supporter, 3 September 1976.)

- 'The inspections have revealed no evidence that at the stocking densities currently practised in the industry, the birds do not generally have sufficient room to turn round, stretch their wings or are otherwise suffering any unnecessary pain or distress.' (Oddly worded letter from MAFF to a supporter of Chickens' Lib, January 1978.)
- 'The number of occasions when the welfare of birds in battery units has been found to be unsatisfactory is extremely small, and in all such cases the producer concerned has responded to welfare advice with the result that any problems have been speedily resolved.' (Letter from the Minister's Private Office to Chickens' Lib, 24 February 1978.)
- 'Concerning feather pecking and cannibalism, birds in cages quickly form a stable group with dominance established. Birds in large numbers in more extensive groups find it harder to form established social groups. Those groups will form and re-form, which can lead to feather pecking and cannibalism.' (Letter from MAFF Animal Health Division to Chickens' Lib, 31 August 1984.)
- 'Providing the recommendations set out in the Code are observed, we believe the welfare interests of battery hens and broiler chickens will be safeguarded ... Our view is, therefore, that existing arrangements already provide considerable protection for the welfare of battery hens and broiler chickens.' (Letter from MAFF to Chickens' Lib, 21 January 1987.)
- 'You will, no doubt, be pleased to hear that [a MAFF veterinary inspector] was satisfied that there was compliance with Welfare Codes at the time of his visit and that the requirements of the Welfare of Livestock (Intensive

Units) Regulations 1978 were fully met.' (Letter from MAFF to Chickens' Lib, 4 September 1987, which refers to a broiler unit containing over 80,000 birds in one shed.)

'NO UNNECESSARY PAIN OR DISTRESS'?

On 24 October 1983 Chickens' Lib visited a farm in Derbyshire where conditions were found to be horrendous. The visit was a random one, and there was no attempt to prevent the public from seeing the true state of the hens, indicating perhaps that the farm was not unusual in its standards of husbandry. Thousands of near-featherless hens co-existed with the decomposing carcases which littered the battery shed's floor, while a face mask hung at the entrance – clearly the fumes within the shed were likely to overpower any worker who ventured in unprotected. In a nearby barn thousands more battery hens lived in squalor and semi-darkness. Following Chickens' Lib's strong complaints, Mrs Wilson, a MAFF veterinary inspector, visited the farm, yet 'no evidence of unnecessary pain or unnecessary distress was found'.[3] Two weeks later, as a result of further complaints, Mr Robson, MAFF's local Divisional Veterinary Officer made a further inspection. His findings were predictable, for 'he also reported that there was no evidence of unnecessary pain or unnecessary distress being caused to the livestock in the units.'[4] Shortly after this, an intrepid supporter of Chickens' Lib succeeded in buying two dozen hens from this very farm, one of which features in a state of shocking nakedness on posters which have been used by animal rights campaigners world-wide.

On the subject of feather loss in battery hens (now accepted as a guide to bird welfare) MAFF has been quick to put forward ingenious explanations for the near-naked state of many battery hens approaching the end of their 'useful' lives:

'The hardy breeds of birds usually kept on free range are

normally more heavily feathered than hybrids which have been evolved for intensive systems under conditions of controlled environment,'[5] and:

'The degree of feather loss in caged poultry may be due to various factors including diet, temperature, colony size, strain of bird, cage design and length of period in lay.'[6]

Regarding smells from intensive poultry units, MAFF officials have been evasive, apparently failing to make the connection between highly offensive smells and poor animal husbandry:

'As I explained to you in my letter of June 16 1981 the State Veterinary Service has no authority to investigate smells. This is quite clearly a matter for the Environmental Health Department of the local authority,'[7] and:

'Many industries, including the agricultural industry, create smells which, although some people may find them overpowering, are in no way connected with problems of animal welfare.'[8] MAFF has chosen to support the popular farming view that those objecting to the smells created by intensive farming methods are 'townies' who can't face up to the real world of agriculture, choosing to live in a picture book fantasy world. However, anyone in a position to compare the strong but sweet smells of animals living with fresh air and clean bedding with the vile stenches emanating from many factory farms can appreciate the flaw in MAFF's reasoning.

SPACE ALLOWANCE: A CASE OF CONFUSION

MAFF has also been guilty of what seems to amount to deliberate obfuscation. In Code Number 3 for Domestic Fowls (applicable from 1971–1987) the recommended floor space for battery hens was described as follows; '3 or more lightweight birds per cage – 39.1 kg/m^2 (8lb/ft^2). 3 or more heavier birds per cage – 44 kg/m^2 (9lb/ft^2).' In the same Code a 4" trough space was recommended 'irrespective of the number of birds per cage'. Needelss to say, perhaps, farmers, rather than weighing their birds precisely (or at all) and grappling with the mathematical complexities of the Code, would put four birds in a cage with a 16" frontage, five to a cage measuring 18" by 20", and so on. However, MAFF wanted no truck with such simple calculations;

'With your letter you sent a sheet of paper whose dimensions you state represent the living space allotted to four battery hens, but the Ministry has no evidence that cages of that size are widely used. In fact cages of many varying dimensions are available to producers, and they can use any they consider suitable provided the choice they make does not cause suffering to the birds housed. The suitability of a cage of any given dimension will depend on the size and strain of bird housed.'[9] One wonders how many battery units this particular Private Secretary had entered.

Despite MAFF's optimistic hope that farmers would prove themselves mathematical wizards when stocking their cages, this was not to be, and for years this aspect of Code Number 3 was disregarded, with hens being stocked at the rate illustrated by Chickens' Lib's sheet of paper! On 9 May 1986 Ms Pittman of MAFF's Animal Health Division 11A admitted: 'The floor area of 562 sq cms which I gave as an example was based on the assumption of an average bird weight of 2.2 kg. The figure of 460 sq cms that you quoted is I believe nearer the average space allowance allotted in the UK.' In other words, while codes rather than regulations existed British farmers had been ignoring the recommended space allowance, aided and abetted by MAFF officials who probably couldn't themselves translate the obscure table of figures into birds per cage. Now the UK has bowed to EEC pressure and agreed to a minimum stocking density of 450 sq cms per bird, so the lot of the British battery hen may be even worse under the new 'welfare' regulations.

OFFICIAL POLICY ON INSPECTIONS AND PROSECUTION

MAFF's State Veterinary Service is admittedly seriously understaffed. Out of some 600 State Veterinary Officers (SVOs) only approximately 425 are field officers, visiting farms (September 1988 figures). Since there are around 210,000 farms in Britain, many of them holding some livestock, their task is clearly a hopeless one. In 1985 'some 6,000 visits were made by SVOs to livestock holdings to advise specifically on animal welfare matters.'[10] To its shame, MAFF seems bent on ensuring that its puny number of welfare visits are as ineffectual as possible, for its avowed policy is to give warning of impending inspections. The usual four or five days' notice farmers receive is all that is needed for guilty ones to carry out massive cleaning-up operations – burning 'deads', culling ailing birds and removing piled-up droppings. One farm visited by Chickens' Lib was given a clean bill of health following a 'welfare' visit just five days after the pressure group's initial complaint, when dozens of cages had been found to contain long-dead birds. Chickens' Lib had purchased one bird with a leg permanently askew, the damage caused by an injury sustained months earlier, as a subsequent veterinary certificate made clear. Despite representations from Chickens' Lib and the RSPCA (whose officers were refused entry) no MAFF vet could be found to visit immediately, and a weekend elapsed before the farmer was given the good news that nothing was amiss.

Despite years of lobbying by welfarists against pre-arranged welfare inspections, MAFF's mind is made up: 'As you will already know from previous correspondence the Ministry's policy is to give farmers notice of Welfare visits and this remains unchanged. The reason for this is to ensure that the farmer is present when the visit is made. Most welfare problems can be corrected by simple on the spot advice and if the farmer were not present to receive this, the visit would be wasted.'[11] The implied scenario, of farms containing many thousands of birds where the owner cannot be found, is indeed a disturbing one, though not in my experience typical. And if one farm should be found to be unattended, there would surely be a neighbouring farm which would benefit from inspection and advice. MAFF should no more give advance warning than do Trading Standards Officers when they go about their duties. Regrettably, no confidence can be felt in the effectiveness of these rare MAFF visits. In May 1983 D. J. Evans, at that time the Divisional Veterinary Officer at Leeds, wrote:

'Thank you for your letter of 3 May about a battery unit in ——, Huddersfield. The information you have provided will be investigated and I should like to thank you for bringing the matter to our attention.'[12] Four years later, almost to the day, Chickens' Lib bought five severely defeathered and wretched hens from a Yorkshire market, and they provided moving material for the video 'Sentenced for Life'. These birds were traced back to the same unit near Huddersfield . . .

We have seen in the previous chapter that MAFF's record on prosecutions of poultry keepers is remarkable. A memorable under-statement came from the desk of John Williams, Leeds' Area Divisional Veterinary Officer who wrote as recently as 22 March 1988: 'We do not routinely use prosecution as an instrument of first resort.' However, it does appear that DVOs are given some discretion at local level as to when to take action. In 1986 a secretarial error ensured that a MAFF internal circular (Animal Health Circular 85/83) addressed to all MAFF veterinary staff fell into Chickens' Lib's hands (or, to be more precise, dropped through the letter box of one of its surprised supporters). It proved to be a revealing document, giving MAFF DVOs permission to decide whether or not to pursue a prosecution, with the proviso that information about 'politically sensitive' cases should be 'quickly passed to HQ'. (A phone call from Chickens' Lib to MAFF established that the battery system is ranked as politically sensitive.)

The circular points out that 'Prosecutions will continue to be taken after persuasion and advice have failed and there is no foreseeable improvement in the situation; *or where there is flagrant disregard of welfare legislation*' [my italics]. One is left to wonder why at least some of the cases of horrific ill treatment which have been brought to the attention of MAFF by welfarists are not seized upon by MAFF officials at regional level, for there is little doubt that more prosecutions would improve on-farm conditions swiftly and dramatically. As it is, it is left to pressure groups and charities to put pressure on the industry, with only the most meagre and grudging and, it would seem, ineffectual support from the public body whose job it is to protect Britain's farm animals from abuse.

On a lighter note, the misdirected circular advises MAFF officials how to deal with demonstrators: 'Demonstrations by welfare organisations need to be handled with care. In the case of extreme welfare groups immediate police assistance must be requested. Other groups should be treated with tact so as not to destroy goodwill and credibility . . . At demonstrations, small local TV company video cameras are unobtrusive and staff should be instructed to stay away from office windows, even if the demonstrators invite this by wearing fancy dress. A film of laughing faces at a window could make "good" media film for a news report.' And so on . . .

THE NFU CONNECTION

The catalogue of MAFF's failings on welfare matters is seemingly endless, and the blame for the relentless growth of factory farming must rest with the Ministry which, as we have seen, has been pleased to defend intensive systems to the last ditch. By why does MAFF do all it can to promote and sustain cruel and unacceptable systems?

It would seem that the close relationship between MAFF and the National Farmers' Union (NFU) accounts for an otherwise inexplicable state of affairs. On 28 July 1988 Sir Richard Body MP submitted the following written Parliamentary Question: 'To ask the Minister of Agriculture, Fisheries and Foods, whether he will give a list of his advisory committees, stating in each case how many members are also members of the National Farmers' Union.' Donald Thompson, on behalf of the Minister, replied: 'The main advisory bodies sponsored by my Department are listed in "Public Bodies 1987" of which a copy is in the library. Complete information as to how many members are also members of the National Farmers' Union is not readily available.'

In all, forty such advisory committees are itemised. Not only are members likely to be drawn from the NFU, but from companies with interests in promoting drugs — the Veterinary Products Committee being an obvious example of a committee where members' self-interest might prevail. In his book *Gluttons for Punishment*, James Erlichman writes: '*The Veterinary Products Committee* (MAFF) does the same job to approve and reassess the safety and use of veterinary medicines. Both bodies (ie the VPC and the *Advisory Committee on Pesticides* — ed) vigorously deny that any of their members have direct links with industry — but again there is no obligation upon Ministers to clear the air. The Liberal MP Mr Paddy Ashdown had put down numerous written questions in the House of Commons in an attempt to force disclosure of all commercial links with the Advisory Committee on Pesticides.' Mr Erlichman goes on to describe graphically the nature of these committees: 'In an ideal world there ought to be a clear separation between the watchdogs and the commercial interests they watch on the public's behalf. But in the real world the avenues between academia, industry and government are actually an intricate maze traversed constantly by a relatively small and closely-knit group of men and women. They often perform, interchangeably, all three roles of expert, industrialist and policy maker.'[13]

At poultry conferences it is often impossible to distinguish between industrialists and MAFF officials. At the first such conference I attended I was astonished to discover that he whom I had assumed to be speaking on behalf of the egg industry was in fact a MAFF poultry advisor. First-name relationships abound, and friendly social occasions are shared. Conferences are arranged, the contact numbers for further enquiries being those of local MAFF and NFU offices. 'Award of Merit' certificates for egg quality are issued with MAFF's 'seal of approval' from its ADAS department, but the certificates *are only given to farmers producing Farmgate Eggs*. Farmgate Eggs are laid by hens fed on Farmgate feeds – the research and development for which was conducted at BOCM Silcock's (Europe's largest feed firm) own farm at Barhill, Cheshire. This farm happened to be the first lucky recipient of a MAFF certificate . . .

It is no wonder then that MAFF's record for prosecuting offending poultry farmers is such a disgraceful one. With MAFF being the only body (except in very rare instances) with automatic right of entry to farms, it is of the greatest importance that an appropriate 'distance' is maintained between MAFF and the farming community. Clearly, the difficulties of balancing the delicate relationship between farmers, MAFF veterinary surgeons and MAFF poultry husbandry advisers should not be underestimated. At the moment the attempt is not even being made, and the scene is totally distorted in favour of farmers and at the expense of the animals.

The present situation may well be beyond salvaging; a more radical solution is needed to many of the problems which beset agriculture. The question whether we need a Ministry of Agriculture at all must be asked. Sir Richard Body in his book *Red or Green for Farmers (and the rest of us)* cogently puts the case for total abolition: 'It would be better to abolish the Ministry of Agriculture altogether. Its postwar raison d'être has gone. The days are over when the policy-makers were agreed that we should strive for maximum food production: logically, the days of the Ministry should be over, too. To have a Ministry of seven thousand officials dedicated to the goal of ever higher levels of output has become a menace to our farmers, our countryside and our health ... The abolition of the Ministry of Agriculture would mark our departure from a policy that has done much damage already and, were it allowed to continue, would cause a catastrophe. Its demise would serve as a signal to us all that we had changed direction at last.' Clearly, farm animals are not benefitting from the protection of MAFF, and revelations about that ministry's totally inadequate response to the food poisoning epidemic Britian now faces must surely point to the need for new, impartial and effective agencies to protect consumers and farm animals alike.

Chapter 5
The Backlash

'Witnesses for the company (D B Marshall Ltd, of West Lothian) said that other examples of cruelty by employees included pulling the head off a live chicken and squeezing a live chicken to force out excrement and even its internal organs. Before Mr Frew's dismissal another employee had been accused of squeezing excrement from a live chicken in the direction of a fellow employee ... The tribunal was told it was common practice in the factory for live chickens which had fallen onto the floor to be thrown up the production line to another employee to be restored to their hooks.' *The Daily Telegraph*, 16 October 1986.

Anyone who believes that high standards prevail in poultry processing plants labours under a delusion. Thousands of birds are slaughtered hourly (over 50,000 birds every working day at Marshall's at the time of the above-reported tribunal hearing) and poultry slaughterers have no professional qualifications. The speed of the operation is breakneck: licensed poultry slaughterhouses must employ meat inspectors, who examine approximately 1,200 birds an hour, or twenty carcases each minute. Inspectors work on shifts, as, clearly, concentration could not be maintained throughout a working day. Yet lapses occur. If an inspector loses concentration (or decides to chat to a work-mate) serious diseased conditions may escape his notice, as birds pass him by at the rate of one every three seconds. The noise, stench and stress in huge poultry slaughterhouses are overpowering. Maintenance of sterilisation equipment is often lax, carcases are retrieved from filthy floors and returned to the line without being disinfected, chill room doors are left open ... Crates and lorries bringing in live birds remain contaminated, despite attempts in larger plants to hose them down. The 'shit game', described at the head of this chapter, appears to give pleasure to some employees, as do games of football with live birds and the practice of stubbing out cigarettes in birds' eyes. Bearing in mind the lax hygiene standards in processing plants, the unhealthy condition of many broilers by the time they reach the plants, and the gross cross-contamination which occurs at the time of slaughter, it is not surprising that chicken meat now represents a very substantial health risk to consumers.

SALMONELLA FOOD POISONING

Salmonella food poisoning is at best unpleasant, causing sickness and diarrhoea, and at worst fatal. The very young and old are most at risk, though anyone who eats infected food can be made seriously ill. The salmonella bug is generally destroyed by thorough cooking, but not always in microwave ovens – researchers have described the 'inefficient destruction of bacteria' in microwave cooking, which is notorious for its unevenness: 'food constituents absorb microwave energy with different intensities'.[1] Experiments detailed in the *Journal of Food Science* (Volume 50, 1985) involved turkeys, but the principle will apply, especially in the case of larger birds. Probably the main danger lies in handling raw chicken, then touching, or allowing the meat to touch, other foods, raw or cooked, in refrigerator, shopping trolley or on kitchen surfaces. Needless to say, undercooked chicken is a recipe for disaster.

The number of reported cases of illness in England and Wales caused by *Salmonella enteritidis* increased six-fold between 1982 (1101 cases) and 1987 (6858 cases). By November 1988 over 10,000 such cases for that year alone had been reported to the Communicable Disease Surveillance Centre. (Information supplied by the Public Health Laboratory Service, Communicable Disease Surveillance Centre – unpublished.) An article in *The Lancet* (24 September 1988) pointed to poultry meat and shell eggs as the main sources of contamination. But new figures based on the current USA 'multiplication factor' (reflecting under-reporting) could bring the number of food poisoning cases in the UK during 1988 from *S. enteritidis* PT4 alone to 1.2 million.

The massive nature of the present-day chicken and egg industries must be held responsible for the enormous increase in salmonella food poisoning. In the case of meat-type birds, there are – as we have seen – very few growers farming the 600 million chickens that are reared and slaughtered annually in the UK (1988 figures). The breeding of the stock is done by a handful of large companies, some of which breed, hatch, rear and slaughter. Slaughterhouse waste (blood, feathers, offal, etc.) is often recycled, so parts of infected dead birds may be incorporated into the feed reaching millions of live ones. Though often a carrier disease (the birds harbouring and passing on the bug) *S. enteritidis* phage type 4 is now gaining ground as a disease resulting in illness and death in the birds: 'The effects of *S. enteritidis* PT4 infection dominated the reports of poultry problems in January, according to the veterinary investigation service. The infection was mentioned by seven centres including Newcastle which described an outbreak in which 12,000 out of 54,000 five-week-old broilers became ill and 1,600 birds died. Norwich reported that *S. enteritidis* phage type 4 and "runting and stunting" syndrome are the two most serious problems for the broiler industry at present . . . Lincoln isolated *S. enteritidis* from the joints of 20-day-old broilers which were showing signs of septic arthritis.' (*The Veterinary Record*, 21 May 1988.) Perhaps the emergence of a strain of salmonella which causes high mortality in the birds will give the lie to the opinion expressed in *The Lancet* (24 September 1988) that 'since the bacterium generally causes inapparent infections in the birds it is not of economic importance to the industry and nothing is done about it.' The spotlight must soon turn from eggs to chicken meat. In fact, not only is the intensivism of chicken and egg production to blame – Professor Alan Linton, of Bristol University's Department of Microbiology claims that most growth promoters increase birds' susceptibility to colonisation by salmonellae.[2]

The millions of birds which show no signs of disease, yet are infected with salmonellae, take the bacteria with them to the processing plants, where cross-contamination is massive, the bugs multiplying to infect hitherto 'clean' birds. Tests at the Central Public Health Laboratory's Food Hygiene Laboratory on birds from retail outlets showed 60% of chickens to be infected,[3] though some estimates put the figure much higher. Inadequate hygiene, the scalding process and contaminated machinery (especially evisceration and plucking equipment) all contribute to the scene of fast-breeding bacteria. Clearly, poultry processing plants should be clinically clean and efficient, but in reality conditions fall far short of the ideal.

SALMONELLA FOOD POISONING FROM EGGS

Chicken meat has long been known to be the chief source of contamination by salmonellae, but now it is known that eggs too can harbour the bacteria. It used to be believed that dirty shells accounted for infected eggs, but *The Lancet* speaks of 'compelling evidence' that transovarian infection is now common.[4] This means that the infection may lurk deep inside the egg, so nothing short of extended cooking at a high temperature can ensure its destruction. Soft boiled eggs, poached or fried eggs, just as much as raw ones, may be suspect. Despite this well-documented fact, the Department of Health initially confined itself to warning

NHS caterers and the public to avoid *raw* eggs and *raw* egg products only.

An investigation carried out in 1987 by Peter Chapman at the Public Health Laboratory in Sheffield showed conclusively that the temperature at the centre of size 2 eggs placed in boiling water for four minutes did not rise above 40 degrees C; therefore any salmonellae present in the egg would survive. This figure applied to eggs stored at room temperature. In the case of eggs kept in a refrigerator, the temperature recorded at the centre of the yolk did not rise above 28 degrees C. Peter Chapman's findings were corroborated by the 24 September 1988 Lancet article which concluded: 'Until the poultry industry, the Ministry of Agriculture, and the Department of Health are willing to collaborate to tackle the real underlying cause of the epidemic of *S. enteritidis* PT4, the public will have to put up with their chickens over-cooked and their boiled eggs rock-hard.'

On 3 December 1988 *The Lancet* detailed investigations carried out by several bodies following four outbreaks of *S. enteritidis* PT4 which occurred in Wales during 1988 and implicated food containing shell eggs from hens as the vehicle of infection. One of the offending items had been scotch eggs, and the article concluded: 'Raw egg consumption may therefore be unsafe. Furthermore, temperatures within the yolk of soft boiled eggs have been shown experimentally not to reach bactericidal levels, and the outbreak data presented here suggest that scrambled eggs, hard boiled eggs and scotch eggs may be sources of infection.'[5]

(Ironically, larger eggs, so favoured by the consumer, are a more dangerous commodity from the point of view of salmonella contamination. Being larger, they heat through more slowly than small eggs, and the shells are thinner, making the likelihood of cracked shells (which can let in contamination from faeces) greater; 'The shell is not impervious to salmonellae ... Penetration may also be aided by cracking or abrasion of the shell, and by poor cuticle layer formation, both of which are common features of battery-produced eggs.'[6]

On 16 December 1988 national newspapers carried a full page statement from the Government: 'Eggs. The Facts.' However, the Chief Medical Officer, Sir Donald Acheson, failed to give adequate warning to the public, though the statement in no way denied that eggs can make people ill, sometimes fatally. The advice opened with the words: 'For *healthy people* there is very little risk from eating eggs which are *cooked*, however you prefer them – boiled, fried, scrambled or poached.' Many of the reported cases of *S. enteritidis* from eggs have *not* involved raw eggs, and *have* involved schoolchildren and young and middle-aged adults – hardly those in 'at risk' categories.

CONTAMINATED FEED

The third main source of contamination is feed, either home produced or imported. Proteins of animal origin (meat and bone, fish meal, or, as mentioned earlier, blood, feathers and offal) are responsible for the contamination. An article in *The Veterinary Record* (2 November 1985) blamed Indian bones and Chilean fish meal. The Protein Processing Orders (1981) were designed to ensure the wholesomeness of home produced and imported feed ingredients. Theoretically, compounders frequently found to be making up contaminated feed risk having their licences revoked. It would seem that the Orders have had little effect. The article concluded: 'The Orders have not yet achieved any conclusive reduction in the level of contamination of either imported or domestic protein.' Can this be yet another case where the powers that be (in this case MAFF) have no wish to rock the boat, by taking action which might seriously inconvenience a section of the poultry industry – the feed firms? Jim Reed, Director-General of the UK Supply Trade

Association, laid 'a share of the blame' at the door of the Ministry of Agriculture when he told *Farmers' Guardian* (2 December 1988): 'The Ministry introduced the Protein Order which was aimed at maintaining the hygiene standards of proteins such as meat and bone meal. But it has been very badly policed, and we suspect that this is a major factor which might have lead to the present crisis'.

Since it started making checks on feed in 1982, MAFF has found 213 poultry feed processing plants to be contaminated by salmonella, some of which were shown to be infected repeatedly. None has been prosecuted, and production and distribution had, until 1989, never been halted. Small wonder that much, if not most, of British egg production is infected with salmonella, to echo Edwina Currie's memorable words.

THE COST OF SALMONELLA POISONING

The cost to the consumer from salmonella food poisoning is high in terms of suffering – severe bouts of sickness and diarrhoea can leave the patient weak for months, and can kill – and in financial terms too. In the USA, 'medical costs and lost productivity from acute intestinal infectious diseases amount to a minimum of about $23 billion a year.'[7] Many of these 'infectious diseases' are caused by the salmonella and campylobacter bugs, both of which greatly favour chickens as their hosts. Nearer home, a 1987 report stated: 'Poultry-borne salmonellosis is the most common form of foodborne infection in Scotland ... The present study identifies and values the costs of a hospital based outbreak of poultry-borne salmonellosis. Account is taken of costs falling on individuals, the health service and society as a whole. Depending on assumptions made about the value of 'intangibles', the cost of the outbreak is estimated to be between £200,000 and £900,000.'[8]

Perhaps the poultry industry (aided and abetted by

MAFF) would clean up its act more quickly if consumers took it upon themselves to sue suppliers of contaminated food. Chicken *can* be cooked so as to kill off dangerous bacteria (though perhaps not in a microwave oven) but should the consumer be responsible for ensuring that the almost certainly infected chicken in his or her shopping basket doesn't contaminate other food purchases? In the case of eggs the picture is clear. If retailers knowingly sell eggs which *may* be contaminated by the salmonella bug, yet are failing to warn consumers that anything short of hard-boiling the product may make them ill (perhaps fatally), they are surely acting irresponsibly. In the USA, where litigation is commonplace, the costs following a hospital outbreak of salmonellosis from eggs in 1963 exceeded a hundred million dollars, the offending hospitals being held liable.[9]

Ironically, British holiday makers' desire for familiar food is ensuring that they don't necessarily 'get away from it all' even when abroad. Reported cases of salmonella food poisoning picked up by the British in Spanish holiday resorts are turning out to be of the British type. I know of one poultry processing plant which exports large quantities of chickens to Spain, expressly for the UK tourist trade . . .

In July 1975 the Zoonoses Order came into force. (A zoonotic disease, or zoonosis, is a disease transmissable directly or indirectly from animal(s) to humans.) The Order states: 'The following organisms, being organisms which, when carried in animals or poultry, constitute in the opinion of the Ministers a risk to human health, are hereby designated for the purposes of section 1 of the Act of 1972:

a) organisms of the genus Salmonella
b) organisms of the genus Brucella.'

Under the heading 'Infected Places' the Order demands: 'Where a veterinary inspector knows or has reasonable grounds for suspecting that there is or has been in any place an animal or bird in which a designated organism is or was present, or the carcase of such an animal or bird, or a product derived from such an animal or bird, he may by notice served on the occupier of that place declare it to be an infected place under section 10 of the Act of 1950 for the purpose of this order.'

With salmonella bacteria present in almost every chicken, fresh or frozen, expediency now rules, and the Zoonoses Order, drawn up with the intention of protecting human health, is apparently ignored. Antibiotics and yet more antibiotics are being used to treat salmonella infection when it appears as a disease, in poultry or humans, while in another attempt to paper over the cracks, 'it is suggested that irradiation of poultry-meat may be the only effective method of reducing the public health problem of poultry-borne salmonellosis.'[10]

CAMPYLOBACTER FOOD POISONING

'The most potent breeding ground for campylobacter organisms which affect man seems to be intensive broiler chicken units, where the birds pick up infection easily. Bird performance seems to be unaffected but surface contamination of fresh and frozen carcases is widespread at the slaughter and processing stage.'[11]

Campylobacter food poisoning is a particularly unpleasant disease renowned for the production of acute abdominal pain and profuse diarrhoea. 'In severe cases grossly bloody stools are common, and many patients have at least one day with eight or more bowel movements. Most patients recover in less than a week, but 20% may have a relapse or a prolonged or severe illness.'[12] 'A small yet significant minority of patients ... suffer complications: children may have *grand-mal* seizures; patients may end up in hospital with 'pseudo-appendicitis'; and others may be incapacitated by reactive arthritis that lingers on long after the acute illness has passed.'[13] Occasionally, if it strikes the very young, the very old, or those already sick, it can be fatal. In Third World countries (to which Britain has been pleased to export intensive poultry technology and stock) the scene is grimmer; '... the prevalence of *campylobacter* in young children in developing countries suggests that it is probably a leading cause of morbidity and mortality in the first two years of life.'[14] (Unpasteurised milk, infected water etc. can also cause campylobacter food poisoning).

In the USA a study conducted at the Johns Hopkins University School of Hygiene and Public Health described 'fully cooked' chicken as a risk factor, and concluded: 'Chicken may be the principle vehicle of transmission for sporadic *Campylobacter* enteritis among college students.'[15] In the UK, a paper entitled 'Food Poisoning – Fact or Fiction?' stated: 'The Communicable Disease Report number 84/52 has given a clear indication that campylobacter infections are now the most significant reported cause of gastrointestinal infection ... It is reported, for example, that at least 80,000 working days may be lost in the United Kingdom per year.'[16] Following comparisons between a food company 'which comprehensively screens all cases of diarrhoea in its workforce' and the incidents of campylobacter infection reported among the general population by the local authority covering the food company's area, it was found that there was a discrepancy of 90%.[17] It must therefore be assumed that only a small percentage of cases are reported, so the suffering caused, and working days lost, through campylobacter are much greater than official figures suggest. In America, researchers talk of the 'vast underreporting' of campylobacter infection.[18]

In 'Food poisoning – Fact or Fiction?' the major role played by chicken in the food poisoning scene is confirmed: 'Meat, and in particular chicken meat, has also been found to be a source of campylobacter infections ... Grant specifically mentioned how kitchen surfaces and butchers' knives could be a major source of infection through cross-contamination.'[19]

Dr Martin Skirrow of Worcester Royal Infirmary states that campylobacter 'can be cultured from most chicken and turkey carcasses sold at retail outlets, not only in Britain, but in the Netherlands, Sweden, Yugoslavia, the USA, Canada, South Africa and Australia.'[20] Dr Skirrow describes how broiler flocks have been found to be colonised by campylobacter within a few days of hatching, but he is not able to explain how infection is introduced into 'the closed environment of the broiler production units.' However it may enter the cycle of chicken production, once in, it is tenacious. In Dr Skirrow's words: 'Freezing of carcasses causes some reduction in the numbers of campylobacters, but once in the frozen state they can survive for several months. To summarise, we can say that there is no immediate prospect for the prevention of infection in poultry.'[21]

Researchers at the Johns Hopkins University School of Hygiene and Public Health suggest: 'Potential sources of entry of organisms into a flock include infection of new born chicks from older birds, contaminated feed (including partially pasteurised bird feather, offal and blood), or contaminated water.'[22]

Since campylobacters thrive in the warm, filthy and often damp conditions in the broiler units which house almost 100% of all chickens produced in the UK, it is obvious that drastic measures need to be taken to reform a method of food production which endangers public health.

LISTERIA MONOCYTOGENES FOOD POISONING

'Listeriosis, caused by *Listeria monocytogenes*, appears to be increasing in incidence worldwide. The disease is of great concern to the food industry. A recent outbreak in California was linked to the consumption of Mexican-style soft cheese and involved more than 300 cases, 30% of which were fatal . . . Listeriosis should be considered in any febrile patient with neurological symptoms of unknown origin, as well as women with unexplained recurrent miscarriages, premature labour or fetal death. A food source should be the prime suspect if any isolated case or outbreak occurs.'[23] This bacterium can be found in various foods, with chicken providing one of its favourite breeding grounds. Conjunctivitis among poultry workers due to *L. monocytogenes* has been recognised as an occupational hazard since the 1950s.[24] In 1974 W. Kwantes and M. Isaac of the Public Health Laboratory in Swansea presented a paper to the 6th International Symposium in which they reported finding 53% of chickens from a local broiler processing plant to be infected with *L. monocytogenes*. Since the factory processed about six million birds a year, the researchers concluded: 'This factory alone would, therefore, issue over three million birds infected with *L. monocytogenes* per annum. The United Kingdom consumption of chickens is over 300 million per annum and if these are infected at the same rate then *L. monocytogenes* could reach the kitchen of practically every household in the country many times a year.'[25]

By 1988 the British had doubled their consumption of chicken since the time of this investigation, following the boom in 'healthy eating' and fast foods.

Listeriosis is an illness with an unusually long incubation period (it ranges from just a few days to ten weeks) making the condition hard to track down to source. Laboratory tests can establish the presence of *L. monocytogenes*, but the food that infected the patient up to ten weeks previously may remain a mystery for all time, unless outbreaks occur (as happened in the USA and Switzerland) in which a common factor (for example mothers and babies attending the same hospital) makes it possible to establish the 'culprit'. But exceptions occur. In 1988 a case of listeriosis was traced to a chicken bought from a Leeds supermarket. Identification of the infected food was made possible by the combination of a short incubation period and a refuse collectors' strike which enabled the chicken carcase to be retrieved and examined: 'A 31-year-old woman with a 24-hour history of influenza-like symptoms and fever was spontaneously delivered of a non-viable 23-week fetus. Five days before the onset of her illness she had prepared a heated chicken dish from a cooked-and-chilled chicken purchased in a supermarket. The remainder of the chicken had been kept for 3 days in a refrigerator and had been eaten cold in a salad. *Listeria monocytogenes* serotype 4 was isolated from the carcase of the chicken, from fetal and maternal blood cultures, and from fetal necropsy samples, including liver.'[26]

The illness manifests itself as meningitis, septicaemia, miscarriages, still births and abscesses. Those most susceptible to infection include unborn and newly-born babies, pregnant women, the old, alcoholics, and cancer and AIDS patients – in short, anyone who is immunocompromised (ie whose immune system is weakened).[27] J. McLaughlin of the Central Public Health Laboratory, Colindale, London, estimates that apart from those in the above categories, some 10%–15% of seemingly healthy people can also fall victim to the illness.[28]

Jeffrey Farber and Joe Losos of the Bureau of Microbial Hazards in Ottawa reckon that with *L. monocytogenes* 'the recorded incidence rates among humans probably represent only a small proportion of actual cases'.[29]

A picture is emerging of widespread illness being caused, with a death rate of 30% acknowledged *in those cases that are thoroughly investigated*. How many cases are never reported – being accepted as 'ordinary' miscarriages or only-to-be-expected deaths in the old or already sick – can only be guessed at. While figures cannot be quoted for the true incidence of listeriosis, those that are available are not reassuring. The Public Health Laboratory Service for England, Wales and Ireland, reported 259 cases in 1987, contrasting sharply with the 107 cases identified in 1986 and an average of only 42 a year in 1967 – 77 (PHLS, CDSC, unpublished).

Richard Lacey, Professor of Medical Microbiology at Leeds University, suspects that fatalities from listeriosis are higher than is generally believed, since the disease is not notifiable and symptoms can often be attributed to other causes. Professor Lacey (who is also the infection officer for Leeds West Health Authority) is especially concerned that the 'cook-chill' method being increasingly used for preparing and storing meals in hospitals (where those eating the food are, by definition, in a vulnerable state) invites contamination. *L. monocytogenes*, which is known to thrive under refrigeration (doubling its numbers every thirty hours) *is more resistant to heat than the salmonella bug*. Thorough cooking does destroy the bacteria, but in view of the ever-increasing cases of salmonella food poisoning through inadequate cooking there can be no room for complacency!

The fact that *L. monocytogenes* thrives in the refrigerator must give great cause for concern, for cross-contamination of other foods will readily occur when raw meat is stored carelessly, while under-cooked infected meat can become even more dangerous once refrigerated. When Professor Lacey's team from Leeds University tested 21 samples of ready-cooked and chilled meat products bought at supermarkets they found that one chicken labelled 'ready to eat' contained 400 organisms of *L. monocytogenes* per gram of meat.[30] John Kvenberg, head of the foodborne microbiological hazard programme of the US Food and Drug Administration believes that anyone with a compromised immune system could be at serious risk from Professor Lacey's 'ready to eat' chicken. An article in *New Scientist* drew attention to the unpredictable nature of listeriosis: 'Both Lacey and Kvenberg agree that most healthy people can probably eat millions of listeria bacteria without becoming ill, though Kvenberg adds that "there are cases of healthy 18-year-old girls contracting the disease and dying".'[31]

To date outbreaks (as opposed to isolated cases) of listeriosis have been associated with soft cheeses, coleslaw, seafood, raw vegetables and milk, no doubt because these frequently harbour the bug, but are not necessarily cooked; yet the figures for contamination of chickens, which may or may not be cooked and stored properly, must be regarded as highly disturbing.

In December 1988 Professor Lacey carried out an investigation for the Thames Television programme 'This Week'. Filmed by a hidden camera, he bought twenty four refrigerated items, chosen at random, from four Leeds supermarkets. Out of these, six were found to contain listeria, four of them being *ready to eat* chicken dishes.

When 68 'oven-ready' chickens were tested at the MAFF Veterinary Investigation Centre in Weybridge in 1976, 14.7% of the samples (which came from shops and supermarkets) were found to be contaminated by *L. monocytogenes*. An article in *The Veterinary Record* describing the tests stressed the importance of detecting the bug at the processing stage: 'The high prevalence of listeria in "oven-ready" poultry recorded by Kwantes and Isaac (1974) and in this investigation underlines the importance in poultry processing of hygiene and of inspection, particularly where the characteristic liver and heart lesions are identified'.[32]

SIXTY PER CENT OF CHICKEN CONTAMINATED

When P. N. Pini and R. J. Gilbert of the Central Public Health Laboratory's Food Hygiene Laboratory in London tested 222 UK and imported soft cheeses and 100 raw (50 fresh, 50 frozen) chickens in 1986 (bought from shops in and around London) they found that 10% of the cheeses were contaminated by *L. monocytogenes*, while a massive 60% of the chickens (both fresh and frozen) harboured the bug.[33]

At around the time of this investigation, David W. Hird of the Department of Epidemiology and Preventative Medicine, University of California-Davis wrote; 'Although some human outbreaks were associated with clinical cases of listeriosis in livestock, the healthy carrier animal remains important as a source of the organism. At present there are no good tools to identify these carrier animals; identification by bacterial isolation is impractical, and serological tests are not entirely satisfactory.'[34]

THE DRUG INDUSTRY CONNECTION

Alongside the inevitable diseases of intensification caused by factory farming, a thriving industry has established itself to market the drugs and growth promoters which help to reduce mortality and downgrading, and boost profits. For secondary infections *in poultry alone*, 44 available antibiotics, from fourteen different drug companies, are listed in *Poultry World's* 1988 Disease Directory.

The dangers arising from the over-use of antibiotics are recognised by leading scientists. Alan Linton, Professor of Bacteriology at Bristol University's Department of Microbiology, states: 'It must be appreciated that antibiotic resistance arises in bacteria as a natural phenomenon. The rate at which it occurs is in proportion to the amounts of antibiotics used. Therefore, it follows, that the more antibiotics are used, or misused, the greater the proportion of resistant bacteria will arise in the individual bird (animal/man) and the environment.'[35]

Antibiotics such as penicillin are widely used in the poultry industry, and may (on veterinary prescription) be incorporated into the feed as a preventative measure at the rate of 20g/tonne for four weeks out of the chickens' seven week 'lifetime'. Should infection strike, the dose would be increased for a few days, to 200g/tonne. The former, preventative, dose may sound reassuringly minute, but Professor Linton stresses that his research has recently shown that antibiotics incorporated into the feed at levels as low as five parts per million can still select for antibiotic resistant bacteria. This means that antibiotic resistant organisms such as *E. coli* (a common cause of disease among broilers) will be selected and may transfer resistance to gut pathogens such as salmonella and campylobacter, in turn rendering them resistant to the antibiotics that may be indicated in the treatment of a sick person.

In December 1983 a letter appeared in *The Veterinary Record* signed by four scientists from the Central Public Health Laboratory (Division of Enteric Pathogens) and stating that a strain of salmonella (*S. typhimurium*) had appeared which is resistant to the antibiotic gentamicin: 'The appearance of gentamicin resistance in *S. typhimurium* from poultry is particularly disturbing since chicken-associated phage types are becoming increasingly important in human food poisoning in Britain'.[36] Earlier that year, an outbreak of *S. typhimurium* in a Scottish hospital had proved to be resistant to six out of eleven antibiotics (Dr. R. Hardie, Communicable Diseases Scotland, Weekly Report 1985, vol 19, no. 46, pp 7–11).

The Veterinary Record's 'Comment' (5 October 1985) said that 'It is clear from anxiety expressed in correspondence and comment in recent issues of *The Veterinary Record* that veterinary surgeons are under considerable pressure to prescribe antibiotics; it is also apparent that illicit supplies are available in some areas.' It should be remembered that some veterinary surgeons have chosen to work in drug companies, where competition between companies is keen and the desire to restrict the use of drugs nil. If the dangers of ever-increasing antibiotic resistance are to be lessened, radical changes must be effected which will make the overuse of drugs unnecessary and the presence of a black market in farm animal drugs redundant.

When conditions are healthy, drugs regarded by the intensive industry as essential are no longer needed. Coccidiostats (sometimes in the form of antibiotics) are used

100% in the intensive broiler industry and by free range producers such as Moy Park (more of which in chapter six). The veterinarian G. S. Coutts writes: 'Young, closely confined birds are mainly affected and it is no exaggeration to say that were it not for timely research into [coccidiosis], which has resulted in the development of effective preventative and curative products, present methods of keeping poultry under intensive systems would never have become a practical proposition.'[37] He also mentions that intensive poultry farmers will be unlikely to notice the first signs of coccidiosis (droppings containing blood) 'in the reduced light of the modern poultry house'.[38] Richard Guy, of the Real Meat Company, told me he uses no coccidiostats when rearing free range chickens, and has no problems with the disease.

The nation's health is now at risk to an unprecedented degree from many pollutants, not least those caused by factory farming methods. A huge proportion of Britain's farm animals (around 99% of all poultry) are living in slum conditions, while, because of our greed and lack of compassion, their sufferings are becoming our own. In one sense, justice is being done.

Chapter 6
A Better Future

> 'When do we say enough is enough and either agree to pay more for techniques which do not cause suffering, or forego the product altogether? If change can only be achieved through regulations we mustn't be afraid of making them. Social history is, after all, full of laws which have been made to prevent people using the cheapest methods of doing things.' Ruth Harrison, Hume Memorial Lecture, London, 26 November 1987.

I have described the grossly inhumane conditions endured by Britain's battery hens and broiler chickens (just two kinds of farm animals to suffer at the hands of the twentieth century revolution in animal husbandry methods) and hoped to imply the unhealthy nature of an intensive poultry stock keeper's job. I have attempted to show that modern systems which involve keeping many thousands of animals together in conditions unsuited to their species are illegal, and that such systems have encouraged the escalation of diseased states, many of which threaten human health and lives. I have suggested that those who might be assumed to be going about their business of ensuring the welfare of farm animals (Ministry of Agriculture officials and veterinarians) are manifestly failing to do so. The scenario is grim, and the weight of animal suffering both past and present enormous. But what of the future?

The animal welfare/rights movement has taken the lid off this particular Pandora's box, exposing the crimes that are being committed against the humblest of farm animals, the chicken. As consumers become more informed about the source of their 'farm fresh' eggs and 'healthy' white chicken meat they feel a mounting unease, while those scientists and doctors increasingly concerned about a potentially lethal backlash from the over-use of antibiotics, and the diseases that can be passed from poultry to humans, continue to voice their concern to a public and media more ready to listen. Farmers, the people who have enabled the dreams of food technologists, poultry scientists, drug companies and civil servants to come true, are failing to make the profits they had hoped for. Only MAFF officials, drug companies and certain veterinarians seem content, and this is to be expected. MAFF has been responsible more than any other body for promoting factory farming methods at the expense of sustainable and humane ones: civil servants whose life work it has been to persuade farmers to produce more and more intensively, and to defend their Ministry's policies come hell or high water, are unlikely to be in a hurry to point accusing fingers at themselves. Drug companies which specialise in 'animal health products' – that is, drugs to keep farm animals alive and producing *despite* the squalor of their surroundings (and the veterinarians who prescribe and sell those preparations) stand to make substantial losses from the introduction of systems which do not rely on routine dosing to keep productivity figures healthy. But despite opposition from the policy makers and the profit sharers, progress towards a more humane future for poultry is being made, albeit painfully slowly. These following examples of current attitudes may help to form a picture:

(1) In 1980 the RSPCA made the following statement in its memoranda submitted to the House of Commons Select Committee which investigated 'Animal Welfare in Poultry, Pig and Veal Calf Production': 'It is crucial to the whole discussion of welfare issues to place firmly on record the Society's total opposition to the battery cage and its insist-

ance that humane alternatives are introduced with as little delay as possible.'[1]

(2) Members of this same Select Committee reported at the conclusion of the 1980-81 session: 'Despite the conflicting arguments our conclusion is clear: we have seen for ourselves battery cages, both experimental and commercial, and we greatly dislike what we saw.'[2]

(3) Some (though not enough) Church men and women have spoken out against what they see as a crime against creation. In 1981 Dr Robert Runcie, Archbishop of Canterbury, wrote: 'Many people have written to me on the subject of hens in battery cages and veal calves in crates. Of course these systems of extreme confinement are to be abhorred . . . History has repeatedly shown that when man exploits his fellow creatures for immediate gain it rebounds on him eventually and leads to spiritual poverty. In the end, lack of regard for the life and wellbeing of an animal must bring with it a lowering of man's own self-respect: "Inasmuch as ye do it to these the least of my little ones ye do it unto me!" '[3]

(4) The Farm Animal Welfare Council, an independent advisory body set up in 1979 by the Minister and the Secretaries of State for Scotland and Wales, 'has been given the responsibility of keeping under review the welfare of farm animals on agricultural land, at markets, in transit and at the place of slaughter. It advises Agriculture Ministers of any legislative or other changes that may be necessary'.[4] In its assessment of egg production systems, published in September 1986, the FAWC concluded in the section on battery hens: 'The birds may be subject to chronic discomfort.'[5]

(5) Euro MP Richard Simmonds organised, with the Agriculture Committee of the European Parliament, a public hearing on the welfare of pigs, poultry and veal calves. Following the hearing a report with recommendations was published in which a call was made for an end to extreme

systems (including the battery system) and more work on alternatives.[6]

We saw in Chapter 3 some of the evidence gathered over the last two and a half decades in poultry research centres pointing to the adverse effects (both physical and mental) suffered by battery hens from their confinement. It is now true to say that the battery system is under fire from unbiased poultry scientists as much as from the welfarists who, until just a few years ago, were regarded by many as cranks. Encouragingly, research sponsored by government and industry is now under way into various aspects of farm animal welfare. Funds for such research would not have been forthcoming but for the sustained pressure from animal welfare groups over the last twenty years or so.

By contrast with the battery system, the intensive broiler chicken industry has been able to produce chickens by the billion with no questions asked, the system remaining virtually unchallenged on welfare grounds until a few years ago. You will note that points one to five above make no reference to broilers. But now both MAFF and the industry are becoming nervous. At the 1988 European Poultry Fair MAFF's Parliamentary Secretary, Donald Thompson, was reported to have warned farmers that the welfare lobby would widen its attack to include broilers, turkeys and ducks.[7] Colin Watson, wearing the hats of Sales and Marketing Director of Marshall Food Groups and Chairman of 'British Quality Chicken', has spoken of the 'uncertainty' surrounding new investment in broiler chickens as stemming from 'problems about animal welfare and such minority groups as Chickens' Lib; publicity about Salmonella; legislation about nutritional labelling and additives etc.'[8] Broiler farmers and companies like Unigate who hope to cash in on the white meat and fast foods boom are finding it increasingly difficult to obtain planning permission to set up new units, as the NIMBY ('Not In My Back Yard') mentality gains ground among country dwellers who see no reason why their environment should be threatened by noise, smells and pollution.

FREE RANGE EGG PRODUCTION

Free range eggs now account for some 5% of the total UK egg market; this figure represents a marked increase over the last five years. Most supermarkets now stock free range eggs, so there is real choice for the consumer, though the price difference between battery and free range can be around the 35p mark in many supermarkets and health shops. Two major problems dog the free range egg scene. (1) Eggs produced from hens kept in very large flocks, where certain aspects of their living conditions are reminiscent of battery units. (2) Battery eggs being passed off as free range. Let us look at these problems, and their possible solutions.

What is a free-range egg?
When the free range egg boom started in the early eighties, with Marks and Spencer and Sainsbury's beginning to sell free range eggs (as a result of pressure from welfarists) the few existing free range farmers were producing eggs from hens kept in small and usually moveable houses, many using the old 'rule of thumb' of 150 hens to the acre. When farmers began to appreciate the potential of the free range egg market, some, though by no means all, decided to invest in new very large houses holding up to 3,000 birds. Other producers gutted existing battery houses, ripping out the cages and installing nesting boxes and perches.

The wish to retain the apparent advantage of automation (less manpower) has resulted in a reluctance to return to the 'old' ways. Although the hens inhabiting these mega-hen houses have daytime access to the approved acreage (now EEC law, which stipulates a maximum of one thousand hens to the hectare, or 405 to the acre) it is becoming apparent that not all birds classed as 'free range' make good use of the land, indeed some never venture out at all. There are two explanations for this. First, birds are territorial, and in these large buildings several separate territories may be established within the house, with birds becoming nervous of crossing alien territories. This situation can be made worse if there is an insufficient number of popholes. Second, food and water are kept only in the house and hens like to stay near their source of supply, returning to it at frequent intervals throughout the day.

Let us assume that most consumers are picturing hens roaming in grassy fields, coming indoors only to shelter, lay their eggs and roost at night. Assuming that hens are following their instincts, does it matter if people are not getting quite what they had in mind? Certainly, hens kept under good management in very large houses are vastly better off than battery hens, although it is disturbing to note that many free range farmers persist in debeaking their birds, or buying them in ready-debeaked, and some farmers report higher mortality figures for free range hens than for caged ones. Whether the eggs laid by these not-so-freely ranging birds are worth the large premium put on most of them is another matter, for the drawbacks inherent in large hen houses are likely to affect both hens and consumers.

Intensive conditions

Hens kept in large numbers in single flocks are under some stress and diseases are far more likely to spread in units where large numbers of birds breathe the same warm, dusty air in a relatively enclosed space, so the risk of the overuse of drugs to counteract outbreaks of infectious diseases is very real. Birds who spend little time outdoors cannot benefit fully from the variety of health-giving plants which should abound on their range, and from fresh air and sunshine. A study carried out in 1982 at the West of Scotland College of Agriculture indicated that free range hens supplement their feed rations with 'substantial quantities' of grass and other food found in the soil. Martin Pitt, a free range Wiltshire farmer, tells me that a free range hen eats roughly half an ounce of vegetation daily. It is reasonable to assume that hens kept under good systems of management which combine modern advantages – for example improved veterinary treatment, and water supplies which do not freeze in cold weather – with the best of 'old fashioned' free range are going to keep healthy and contented. They will also provide the consumer with an egg which is richer in nutritional value, resulting from a more varied diet, than will those living in semi-intensive conditions.

Even those farmers who have set up very large houses could improve the existing situation by providing their flocks with a 'scratch' feed – that is whole grain – which can be widely scattered at some distance from the house at least once a day. There is even a device available for scattering grain automatically, though it would seem a pity to deny the stock keeper the pleasant job of throwing the grain and watching the birds half-run, half-fly in their eager enjoyment. Outside dispensers for the milled grain and soya which form the staple diet of most laying hens are available. These exclude wild birds, hold large amounts of feed, and can be placed strategically in fields to encourage the hens to roam. But one of the chief disadvantages of large houses is hard to remedy – the problem of contamination of the ground surrounding the house. This is almost inevitable with poultry houses which cannot be moved. Hens spend a lot of their time in the immediate vicinity of the house, wearing away any grass, so quite quickly the area becomes denuded of vegetation, and probably a sea of mud in winter. Scattering gravel around helps, but the risk of land becoming 'fowl sick' is great.

Various designs of small moveable houses are available. One promising compromise between large automated free range houses and the old-fashioned kind (which often held around fifty hens) is the 'Bloomfield Frainger', designed by Berkshire free range farmer Steve Davies and marketed by Challow Products Agricultural Ltd. of Faringdon in Oxfordshire. The house is intended to hold 320 birds, is fully moveable, and its header tank ensures an unfrozen water supply even in severe weather. A smaller version holding around 100 birds is also available. Feed dispensers hold two days' supplies, so chores can be geared to be minimal at weekends, for instance, though naturally birds must be let out, and shut in again at night. Many farmers, like Mr Davies, find that electric fencing deters foxes successfully. Mr Davies reports very low annual mortality figures – around 3%.

Could all UK hens range freely?

There are 211,638 farms in England, Scotland and Wales (MAFF figures for June 1987) and approximately one quarter of farmers keep some poultry. If one in four farmers kept one thousand hens, the national laying flock would be maintained at its present level. Fears have been expressed (by the pro-battery farming lobby) that there is not enough land to accommodate all hens on free range. However, at the moment millions of acres are dedicated to producing unwanted grain crops: 'In 1986 we have a surplus of some seven million tons of milling wheat. Feed wheat is kept in intervention stores in conditions of near secrecy and at a cost which the public is not allowed to be told.'[9] In suitable areas land could be turned over to grassland to support free range hens, which can run with cattle and sheep. Hens can also form part of the cycle of crop rotation, thriving on the remains of the harvest, cleaning up left-over grain. There is no foundation for the belief that there is not enough space for all UK hens to be on free range, but good reason to question farmers' ability to look after them properly.

Egg production used to provide pin-money for the farmer's wife, fitting in well with her life-style. Nowadays, she is likely to be working outside the home, pursuing her own career. Even those tied to the house by small children or for other reasons might be unwilling to brave the elements. Modern intensivism has all but destroyed the relationship stock keepers, male or female, enjoyed with their animals, and this must be fostered again. Many agricultural colleges now run courses in free range management, but the traditional understanding, passed down through the generations, has suffered a rude interruption. If free range hens are not to suffer at the hands of incompetent farmers, many of whom are jumping on the free range bandwagon, often from totally unrelated jobs, it is important that stringent welfare checks form part of the new farming scene.

At the moment over 90% of all egg production goes on behind closed doors and the scope for abuse is enormous. Most free range hens are, by definition, visible to the general public, so extreme suffering such as has been discovered in battery farms, where birds have been starved and neglected mercilessly, would not afford the farmer perpetrating it much popularity with his or her neighbours. However, it would be a naive reformer who thought that a return to free range would solve all problems, and it is essential that the subject of welfare inspections and flock size is given a great deal of thought at the highest level. Existing MAFF arrangements have ensured that many farms escape welfare checks for years, or indefinitely.

The phoney free-range egg
Another problem besetting the development of the free range egg market is that of non-genuine free range eggs. Many farmers and retailers pass battery eggs off as free range, making handsome extra profits on every dozen sold. This dishonesty is by no means rare, and makes the job of promoting free range eggs doubly hard. A survey carried out in 1986 by Birmingham's Consumer Protection Divi-

sion revealed many instances of falsely described eggs. For example, a health food shop was found to be buying in ungraded eggs from an unregistered producer, and selling them as Class A quality free range eggs – both claims being false.[10]

Probably the worst case of a misleading description came to light as a result of an RSPCA prosecution, featured in the BBC2 series 'Animal Squad', when RSPCA officers discovered a scene of death and misery in a near-abandoned battery unit in Leeds. Here a mother and son team was selling eggs produced by any surviving hens (dead ones littered the cages and obstructed gangways) as free range.

These cases were exposed, but how many are not?

Ironically, eggs can look good whatever their source, though flavour, yolk colour and firmness of white are often poor in battery eggs. Yolk colour can be regulated through additives in the feed, using the chemical citranaxanthin, or more natural additives such as certain flower petals. Consequently, eggs lend themselves admirably to dishonest dealings, yet another reason for banning methods of production which are objectionable to many consumers. The Swiss have gone a long way towards solving the problem of phoney free range eggs, developing a scheme whereby genuine free range producers are issued with a quantity of egg boxes appropriate to the number of their laying hens. The Swiss equivalent to the RSPCA was responsible for working out the logistics of the plan, and it reaps a small profit on every box sold – surely an idea for our RSPCA to look into closely?

Alternatives to cages
Various semi-intensive alternatives to the cage system exist, some in commercial use, and some still at the experimental stage. These include the Aviary and Perchery systems. To describe these I can probably not do better than to quote from a letter to Chickens' Lib from Dr Ballantyne, Deputy

Director of Poultry at MAFF's experimental husbandry farm at Gleadthorpe:

'*The Aviary system* increases available floor space by means of additional levels of platforms which are interconnected by ladders. The platforms may be littered but are more traditionally slatted. Ladders are incorporated into the systems for both the bird and stockman's use. Feeders, drinkers and nest boxes are provided at most, if not all, levels . . . *The Perchery system* was developed in Scotland by Michie and Wilson (1984). It consists of several tiers of perches with feeders, drinkers and next boxes at most levels. The floor area surrounding the "perch block" may or may not be covered with litter material. Generally, the perchery designs used for commercial egg production exclude litter, so as to reduce the floor egg problem and minimise the risk of disease, through birds having access to their own droppings.'[11]

Both these systems have been designed to make better use of the volume of space within the building. Both types of houses can form the production method for 'Barn Eggs' or for free range, though of course in the case of the latter, adequate land must be available during the daytime. ('Barn eggs' is a highly misleading name for eggs produced from these buildings – the hopeful consumer conjures up a picture of rural peace, while the true one is more reminiscent of rush hour on the London underground, with hens not only thick on the ground but on every available perch or platform.) Needless to say, the lack of litter severely reduces the birds' ability to exercise natural instincts, though some diseases will be reduced, just as they are in the battery cage. Aviary houses at Gleadthorpe EHF have been forced to close following severe bouts of cannibalism: 'The wide open spaces of the aviary had given the birds too much opportunity in which to beat each other up.'[12] Space there was, in the sense that the birds were not caged, but aggression was rife, in the atmosphere of stress and competition.

A more successful version, using the perchery design, was not without its teething troubles when 'the perch/alighting rail distance of about 2ft did not give the birds time to adjust their flight if they were off target and there had been one or two crashes and broken legs.'[13]

With all the farmland available, it is tragic that poultry boffins persist in developing systems which would require exceptional stockmanship to keep them going with any measure of success (in welfare terms) while government departments search for alternative uses for redundant farmland, ranging from tourism to golf courses.

The Getaway Cage

Another favourite with those with an undying commitment to cages is the so-called 'Getaway' cage. First designed in the early '70s, it is basically a larger cage with scope for perches, nesting boxes and dustbathing areas. Scope too for more aggressive behaviour, and without even the benefit of the relative cleanliness of cages. The clouds of dust that would be raised by the more active birds, and the problems of higher birds defecating on lower ones probably ensure the dismal failure of this system, which has engaged the imagination of poultry scientists for nearly two decades.

The Elson Terrace

Gleadthorpe EHF has developed the Elson Terrace, which looks little different from a battery unit, but, like the Getaway cage, allows birds more freedom, though still in a highly congested and therefore stressful situation. Terry Ellener, a farm manager responsible for half a million battery hens remarked on seeing the Elson Terrace: 'It is still a cage, and still gives that enclosed feeling,'[14] while another visitor to Gleadthorpe, Jim Baker (a Suffolk battery farmer), noticed the potentially lethal design of the looped drinking water dispenser: 'It is liable to cause an airlock so that although you have water in the header tank, there is none in the nipple. The result can be disastrous.'[15] Farmers who rely on automation are all too prone to put their trust in it – yet just a few hours without water in a heatwave would result in thousands of birds dead from heat stress.

The Straw Yard
The Straw Yard system is in very limited use in the UK but represents one of the best alternatives to cages from the hens' point of view. It allows daylight and sunshine to be enjoyed while the straw litter is kept dry by an overhanging roof and three covered sides. The south side is open, but netted to exclude wild birds. Here, the stocking density is all-important, for once over-stocked, the birds can be under stress and prone to aggression. The Cambridge School of Veterinary Medicine used to display a straw yard in which the birds were stocked at a density of 3 sq ft per bird, and the hens looked content, and they and the litter in good condition.

FREE RANGE – A HEN'S BIRTHRIGHT

It is often argued by welfarists that the way forward will involve a progression from cages to a variety of alternative systems. This is an attractive standpoint, and on the surface sounds more rational than the more radical call for a full-scale return to free range farming. However, having observed the behaviour of laying hens very closely for some years, I am convinced that they are entitled to life on range, with adequate shelter from rain, wind, snow and sun. I do not believe that the human race has the right to deny another species access to sunshine or even to the less pleasant elements, all of which hens are well equipped to enjoy or withstand.

My small (non-commercial, I'll be the first to admit!) flock of hens has 24-hour access to a fox-proof covered straw yard. Yet when I open their pophole to the orchard they burst out, eager for a new day seeking worms and pecking at grasses, regardless of weather conditions. They will happily choose to get their feathers wet, no doubt weighing up the disadvantages of wet weather against the prospect of worms coming to the surface. But not all of their activities are strictly practical – I sometimes watch my hens dozing in the sunshine, a 'behavioural pattern' shared by humans, to precisely the same end – that of sheer enjoyment. Only snow seriously deters some, though not all, from using the land – in which event a few straw bales spread around outside can provide welcome dry areas.

The 'rational' argument against free range, that activities such as walking (so using up energy!) and preening wet feathers (more energy!) increase feed consumption may seem valid, but should be weighed against the very substantial losses from cracked and broken eggs which abound in batteries. In a study carried out at the West of Scotland College of Agriculture not only were free range hens found to lay more eggs than battery hens over an 80-week period, but the percentage of cracked eggs was 2.2 as against 9.2, in favour of free range.[16] I mention this because there are advantages with free range production which are often overlooked when the sums are being done.

Society owes a huge debt to the millions of battery hens who have suffered untold deprivation in the name of food production – the very least consumers can do is to insist on the best possible life for laying hens in future. It is perhaps true that there may be an initial shortage of people qualified to manage free range units successfully, but semi-intensive systems are equally, or more, open to abuse by mismanagement. Free range, *if properly set up*, to some extent runs itself. Grass regenerates itself, birds can cool themselves by raising their wings or seeking shade; water can be readily available without fear of automatic systems failing; and temperature fluctuations rarely, if ever, kill when there are no ventilation systems to go wrong. Time, money and expertise devoted to research and development of 'Getaway' cages and the like would be better put towards perfecting free range, blending the best of traditional knowledge with technological and veterinary progress. The alarm caused by eggs contaminated by salmonellae has raised more questions than it has answered. At the present time my opinion is that the likelihood of free range hens creating health hazards is small. But this must assume not only good animal husbandry (small flocks, moveable huts and feed free of animal protein) but healthy stock – i. e. chicks. Only time will tell if this is possible.

FREE RANGE CHICKEN PRODUCTION

Is there a humane solution to the problems posed by the intensive chicken industry? Can the UK continue to produce chickens at its present rate (over 600 million a year at the latest count) without causing suffering to the birds, endangering public health and threatening the environment?

Because of its cheapness and availability, the popularity of chicken meat has soared. But as we have seen, mass production has brought with it mass animal misery, public ill health, and the dangerous over-use of antibiotics. Far from being a health food, as the industry and some nutritionists would have us believe, chicken meat provides an unrivalled reservoir of infection.

An inherently unhealthy system
Reducing stocking densities drastically would improve conditions immediately, since the ratio of faeces to litter would be reduced accordingly. If broilers were given twice their present floor space (such 'generosity' would bring the figure to just over one sq ft per bird) their lives would be far more tolerable and the incidence of death from starvation and dehydration reduced, as would the suffering caused by hock

burns, breast blisters etc. However, modern broiler chickens' built-in obesity would still tell against them. A free range chicken farmer in Sussex who rears both broiler type chickens and the much slimmer Poulets Noirs table birds popular in France told me that, even on range, the former literally carry with them the burden of their too-rapid growth, many suffering from the same health problems that afflict intensively-reared birds. Poultry scientists have engineered a defective bird. If humans were expressly bred for their tendency to voracious appetites and obesity, the results would be similar – they would be plagued by heart attacks, arthritis etc, even if living in a healthy environment.

A more generous space allowance alone would merely put up the price of chicken, while the problem of disease would persist. Broiler houses would remain breeding grounds for salmonella, campylobacter etc, and the terrors and injuries associated with mass catching and transport would not be lessened. Unpopular though this message may be with the keen consumer of chicken meat, if gross cruelty is to be avoided, chicken production must return to the small scale, though such a change would require a huge increase in the number of stock keepers, and chicken would cease to be the cheapest of cheap meats.

Could British chickens range freely too?
Where would all the chickens be accommodated, were they no longer crammed into huge, gloomy, stinking sheds? When doing the calculation, it must be remembered that, as things stand at present, at any one time there are approximately 100 million birds being reared on a little more than 1000 farms, with each farmer or company putting through five and sometimes six 'crops' a year. For a moment let us assume that the stocking density of 4000 birds to the acre currently adopted by the biggest supplier of free range chickens in the UK (Moy Park Ltd) is a good one.

This figure requires approximately a quarter of a million acres of suitable (i. e. well drained and situated) farmland, to allow the UK's present national flock to be on range. Clearly, with the farmer putting through several 'crops' a year, much more land would need to be available to allow for rotation, to avoid the build-up of disease. If we multiply the figure by six, it comes to 150,000 acres – approximately half of 1% of Britain's total farmland, or an area the size of the county of Cleveland.

The operation of cramming birds into dimly-lit sheds, dosing them with growth-promoters and therapeutic antibiotics to counter all the ills brought on them by slum conditions, and, seven weeks later, turning them out listless, obese, and often sick and crippled – all this requires one kind of 'stock keeper'. The alternative way – rearing birds and allowing them to enjoy freedom, fresh air and good heath – requires another. A far greater number of stock keepers would be required under extensive systems, and though this would provide pleasant, healthy outdoor employment, it would also put the price of chicken beyond the reach of most peoples' purses. As with free range egg production, there might well be a shortage of the right sort of farmers. Free range farming is not just a question of dealing with suppliers on the telephone, seeing in the goods, checking on automatic equipment and removing the deads: those farmers who are now making their living in the intensive industry may not be the same people who would be interested in, or capable of, running free range farms.

The effluent problem
If all chickens were on free range, the volume of used litter would still be very considerable. However, if chickens formed only a small part of each farm's production, the litter could be valuable as fertilizer, and a fair proportion of the droppings would be deposited straight onto the land by the birds on range. 2.5 million tonnes of used litter are

produced annually from intensive broiler units in the UK. Huge mounds of litter are stored on farm land and often contain harmful bacteria (which may remain active for several weeks). The remains of dead birds, attracting rats and flies are now a familiar sight in the countryside. J. McLaughlin, in his 1987 paper *'Listeria monocytogenes*, Recent Advances in the Taxonomy and Epidemiology of Listeriosis in Humans'*,* points to research by Dickgiesser (1980) and Watkins and Sleath (1981) who found that L. monocytogenes can survive 'without significant loss' for weeks and even months in moist and dry environments, and on grassland.

The by-products from a chicken processing industry, intensive *or* free range, must go somewhere, and much is dumped into rivers. In May 1988 Turners Chickens was given permission by the Severn Trent Water Authority to discharge up to 3,640 cubic metres of poultry processing effluent *daily* into the River Trent from Unigate's new chicken factory in Scunthorpe. The factory boasts 'sophisticated' equipment for treating the waste, yet such a massive output adds to the burden of what is off-loaded by industry into our rivers and seas. Perhaps a more environmentally damaging picture will emerge when Unigate's fifty-million-birds-a-year complex gets into full swing. The used litter (which Unigate spokesmen choose to call 'organic') will be absorbed by the farmland of Humberside to the tune of 250,000 tonnes annually. What impurities leach into nearby water courses and underground water supplies will emerge later. The apparent advantages of the 1,200 jobs provided by the Unigate development might well be cancelled out by subsequent pollution of water supplies, which may be severely over-stretched by the demands of fifty million chickens drinking some 110 million litres of water annually. Any calculations about processing slaughterhouse waste apply to free range production too, but water consumption on range is much reduced, unless summer temperatures match those maintained in broiler sheds.

Aggression on free range

From the welfare point of view there is a hidden drawback in Moy Park's style of free range chicken production, which must make the above already dubious figures on space allowance (4,000 birds to the acre) useless as a blueprint for humane chicken farming. Moy Park is the biggest producer of free range chickens, supplying many supermarkets, including Marks and Spencer. All its free range chickens (Moy Park also grows broilers) are reared on small farms, mostly of between three and eight acres, in Northern Ireland. For the first four weeks, all birds are kept intensively (when such young birds must have warmth and protection from the elements), then transferred to free range farms where they live for a further minimum of four weeks, generally being slaughtered at just over eight weeks of age. It is regrettable that during their very short lifetimes they suffer the trauma of catching and transport twice. What is not apparent to the consumer is that *all Moy Park chickens are female*. Moy Park's explanation for this feature of its production is that female chicks feather up more quickly than males, but since the difference is only three or four days the alternative explanation given to me by a broiler expert, that females are less aggressive, would seem the more plausible one. In broiler sheds, aggression can be controlled by reducing lighting levels drastically. On range there can be no such control. Moy Park stocks at 4,000 birds to the acre – ten times the stocking density laid down in EEC law for laying hens (no rules exist for table chickens) and *nearly twenty-seven times* the traditional free range density of 150 birds to the acre. No wonder aggression might prevail! All males hatched (roughly 50% of chicks) are doomed to the broiler industry, so every Moy Park free range bird has her counterpart living in the squalor of a broiler shed. Should the 'feathering-up' explanation be the correct one, perhaps Moy Park should consider rearing both sexes, and keeping them indoors for the extra few days.

Overstocking causes disease

Coccidiostats (drugs to counter the parasitic disease coccidiosis) are given to most free range birds, as well as to all intensively-kept broilers. But are coccidiostats a vital part of chicken rearing? Peter Curtis of Liverpool University's Department of Veterinary Science states: 'It is possible to rear chickens without anti coccidials if husbandry is very good, relying on therapy for control should the disease appear in the flock',[17] while Dr David Sainsbury of Cambridge University's Department of Clinical Veterinary Medicine writes: 'I know plenty of farmers who never use coccidiostats during rearing'.[18] Once again, the huge and unhealthy nature of the chicken industry is responsible for disease patterns which emerge and demand routine dosing with drugs.

Free range chicken farming along Moy Park lines could partially replace intensive production, but the likelihood of fowl-sick land (necessitating drugs from day-old to a few days prior to slaughter) and the condemning of all male chicks to extermination or to broiler houses make for a less-than-idyllic scene.

Controlling numbers and drug use

In France, a mass-producer of broilers, a scheme exists to keep free range chicken production in the hands of family farms. No more than 4,000 birds may be kept in one house, and no farmer may have more than three houses. Each house must contain a flock of a different age. Similar rules in the UK would guard against the spectre of big business moving in to fill the market now being created by an increasing demand for free range chickens. Legislation should be drawn up stipulating requirements for stocking densities, and these should be based on a quality of husbandry which renders drugs unnecessary. Small mixed farms could happily integrate free range chickens to form a balanced part of their production, using cereals and straw grown on the farm, and accommodating used litter as fertilizer. It is unlikely that much improvement, either on the egg or chicken scene, will come about without the intervention of government, unless consumers mount truly effective boycotts of factory-farmed products; at the moment it is only a small minority of people who question the source of their eggs or chicken meat, though the danger of food poisoning from eggs and chickens may continue to depress sales drastically. Bearing in mind the vast sums of taxpayers' money that have been given in recent years to farms to rip up hedges, drain pastures, and subsidise the stuff of food mountains, it is surely time that public money is channelled into systems which put welfare of animals, and a healthier product for consumers, high on the list. The Farm and Food Society has put proposals to MAFF for welfare subsidies to be paid to farmers operating humane systems but MAFF's response so far has been negative.

All poultry keepers with flocks of over fifty birds should be obliged to register with MAFF, so every regional office would have a complete list of these producers. At present no system exists for ensuring that MAFF is aware of farms: anyone can set up a poultry farm with no obligation to inform the Ministry.

This would ensure that the whereabouts of all commercial flocks in the UK would be known, and checks could be made to assess welfare standards, bearing in mind that one spot check would be worth a hundred, perhaps a thousand, cosy pre-arranged MAFF visits. Indeed, MAFF must not be allowed to retain its stranglehold on welfare visits, having proved itself inadequate on two counts: staffing levels, and the will to prosecute if necessary. Representatives from voluntary bodies (not only the RSPCA) along with local authority officials should be allowed to accompany MAFF vets, or carry out preliminary inspection *without a MAFF presence if needs be*, being issued with passes to ensure right of entry to farm buildings in the company of the owner, without prior notice. This may sound like an unacceptable invasion of privacy, but it must be recognised that farmers should no longer be assumed to *own* animals, as they do tractors, vegetable crops, farm buildings etc, but to be *responsible* for them, along with other bodies. Too often, farmers have proved themselves unworthy of being in sole charge of living creatures.

In addition, the police should be better versed in animal protection laws, and less liable to rely on the RSPCA and MAFF when members of the public report cases of animal abuse. The RSPCA has become the main agency for enforcing animal protection laws, but why should the police automatically defer to a charity?

Helping farmers off the treadmill

These, then, are some of the improvements which could be put into practice without further delay. Sufficient incentives and subsidies must form a central part of any strategy devised to get farmers off the treadmill of intensive egg and chicken production.

The Egg Industry Outgoers Scheme, a 'scheme prepared as part of a long term objective of the British Egg Information Council to improve the position of UK egg producers',[19] has now been rejected as economically untenable, but could be taken up by government. The plan entailed proposals to pay battery farmers the suggested sum of £2 per bird to get out of egg production for a period of at least five years, with the proviso that cages should be destroyed. At a time when the egg industry is in crisis, such a measure would be welcomed by many producers, who are without the benefit of guaranteed prices in the face of overproduction.

Clearly, there must be a run-down period before systems can be outlawed, and this should be worked out for both battery and broiler systems, bearing in mind that a five year run-down on the battery system was recommended by the House of Commons Agricultural Committee as long ago as 1981. Those who, like MAFF's Parliamentary Secretary Donald Thompson, fear that 'any unilateral ban on battery units within the UK would risk a surge of imported eggs from the Continent'[20] might take comfort from article 36 of the Treaty of Rome, which stipulates: 'The provision of articles 30 – 34 shall not preclude prohibitions or restrictions on imports, exports or goods in transit justified on grounds of public morality, public policy or public security: the protection of health and life of humans, animals or plants.' To date, it has not been proved that article 36 is *not* relevant to cruel intensive husbandry systems and it would appear to provide a bona fide reason for banning imports of battery eggs and broiler chicken meat once these systems are outlawed in the UK. Already Switzerland and Sweden are moving towards achieving total bans on battery cages during the 1990s. Furthermore salmonella food poisoning is not confined to the UK, but is a world-wide problem. 'Since 1978 *S. enteritidis* has been increasingly responsible for outbreaks of foodborne disease in Spain . . . Data from the Basque region are similar, *S. enteritidis* being responsible for 78% of outbreaks of known aetiology and egg and egg-based products being the vehicle for 90% of outbreaks caused by salmonella.'[21] Clearly, imported eggs and chickens are likely to threaten the 'health and life of humans' too.

Veterinarians, key figures in the farming scene, have not been noted for their opposition to farming methods which, per se, cause suffering and distress to the animals they may be called upon to treat. Every vet declares on joining the ranks of the Royal College of Veterinary Surgeons that 'my constant endeavour will be to ensure the welfare of animals committed to my care' – a promise open to various interpretations, it must be admitted, but surely not to the one of supporting systems in which the profit motive, or the desire to be socially acceptable to the farming community, overrides concern for animal suffering. When the Reverend Tony Birkbeck, a member of the Farm Animal Welfare Council since 1979, presented the Wooldridge Memorial Lecture on 28 September 1988 to the British Veterinary Association Congress at Lancaster University, he illustrated the difficulties encountered by veterinarians whose loyalties might be to his or her client, MAFF's State Veterinary Service, commercial companies and to the Royal College or the British Veterinary Association. He cited an example: 'Dilemmas arising from dual loyalties can be very real. I know of a situation where, on one hot and humid day, over 2,000 chickens died outside a processing plant. The official Veterinary Surgeon, responsible to the district council under the Poultry Slaughterhouse Act, acts also as consultant to the company. He may be reluctant to make a report that may be used in apportioning blame. The poultry meat inspector has to work there; how tolerable would he find life after giving evidence in court?'[22] We should not be surprised that humans, in all their frailty, often fail to ensure the welfare of farm animals, but we must not accept the status quo as inevitable. If we do, we might as well deem acceptable the economic advantages of slavery, child labour and other recent social evils.

Ruth Harrison, in her Hume Memorial Lecture, suggested that consumers should be prepared to pay more for humanely-produced animal products or 'forego the product altogether'. There is a growing number of people who believe that the best way to avoid contributing to animal suffering is to live, as far as possible, without exploiting animals for any purpose. To these people, the act of satisfying the demands of their taste buds does not seem a good enough reason for eating animals, or animal products. (Cannibals presumably derive much pleasure from the taste of human flesh!) The 'Living Without Cruelty' concept is gaining ground daily. But until the time comes when alternatives to animal-derived food are accepted by society, or until laws are passed to prohibit the farming of animals for food, it is essential that systems which cause suffering to animals are replaced by more humane ones, with all speed.

References

CHAPTER 1: BATTERY EGG PRODUCTION

1. National Farmers' Union; *Quarterly Egg Producers Bulletin*
2. MAFF ADAS Press Release, 14 September 1987
3. MAFF ADAS leaflet 568
4. *Ibid.*
5. MAFF ADAS leaflet PR 54
6. MAFF leaflet 703: *Codes of Recommendations for the Welfare of Livestock – Domestic Fowls*
7. Michael J. Gentle and Fiona L. Hill; *Physiology and Behaviour* Vol. 40 pp. 781–783
8. R. N. Kay, B. Sc, MRCVS; *Poultry Meat Inspection Training Manual* (Derbyshire Dales District Council)
9. MAFF ADAS leaflet 540
10. MAFF ADAS leaflet (see n. 6)
11. M. J. Gentle in the *WPSA Journal*, Vol 42 No. 3, October 1986
12. MAFF leaflet 703 (see n. 6)
13. Letter to *Sutton and Epsom Planet*, 12 February 1988
14. Interview on Central TV's ECO programme, 25 April 1988
15. *Poultry World*, September 1988 – account of prosecution of Keighley butcher Adrian Hargreaves
16. MAFF ADAS; *Poultry Technical Information*, No. 13
17. Letter from MAFF to Chickens' Lib 19 May 1983
18. *Broken Bones in Chickens, I: Handling and Processing Damage in End-of Lay Hens*. Drs. N. G. Gregory and L. J. Wilkins, AFRC, Institute of Food Research, Langford, Bristol, 1989
19. Information given to Chickens' Lib during an interview with the management of a leading processing plant on 26 November 1984

CHAPTER 2: THE BROILER CHICKEN INDUSTRY

1. Ruth Harrison, *Animal Machines* (Stuart Publications 1964)
2. Letter from Jim Holton (National Farmers' Union National Broiler and Breeder Specialist) to Chickens' Lib, 19 July 1988
3. *Poultry World*, 28 November 1985
4. G. S. Coutts, BVMS, MRCVS; *Poultry Diseases Under Modern Management* (Nimrod Press Ltd, 1987)

5 Trevor Bray, *Poultry World*, 7 March 1985
6 *Poultry World*, May 1988
7 G. B. S. Heath; 'The Slaughter of Broiler Chickens', *WPSA Journal*, Volume 40, No. 2; June 1984
8 *The Daily Telegraph*, 9 May 1988
9 R. N. Kay, B. Sc., MRCVS; *Poultry Meat Inspection Training Manual* (Derbyshire Dales District Council 1987)
10 G. S. Coutts BVMS, MRCVS; *Poultry Diseases Under Modern Management* (Nimrod Press Ltd. 1987)

CHAPTER 3: INTENSIVE PRODUCTION AND THE LAW

1 Letter to Chickens' Lib, 21 January 1987
2 Letter to Chickens' Lib, 1 August 1988
3 Letter to Chickens' Lib, 11 September 1985
4 R. N. Kay, B. Sc., MRCVS; *Poultry Meat Inspection Training Manual* (Derbyshire Dales District Council, 1987)
5 Letter to Chickens' Lib, 21 April 1988
6 Welfare of Livestock (Intensive Units) Regulations 1978, Statutory Instrument No. 1800
7 James Erlichman; *Gluttons for Punishment* (Penguin Special 1986)
8 *First Report from the Agriculture Committee Session 1980–81*; Volume 1, p. 96
9 *Poultry World*, November 1985
10 *Poultry World*, Editorial Comment, 4 February 1982

CHAPTER 4: THE ROLE OF MAFF

1 *The Scottish Farmer*, 25 June 1988
2 Letters to Chickens' Lib
3 MAFF letter to Chickens' Lib, 24 November 1983
4 MAFF letter to Chickens' Lib, 24 November 1983
5 MAFF letter to Chickens' Lib, 15 July 1974
6 MAFF letter to Chickens' Lib, 2 July 1979
7 MAFF letter to Chickens' Lib, 30 September 1981
8 MAFF letter to Chickens' Lib, 16 June 1981
9 MAFF letter to Chickens' Lib, 24 February 1978
10 MAFF letter to Chickens' Lib, 6 October 1986
11 MAFF letter to Chickens' Lib, 7 June 1988
12 MAFF letter to Chickens' Lib, 4 May 1983
13 James Erlichman; *Gluttons for Punishment* (Penguin Special 1986)

CHAPTER 5: THE BACKLASH

1. J. A. G. Aleixo, B. Swaminathan, K. S. Jamesen, and D. E. Pratt; 'Destruction of Pathogenic Bacteria in Turkeys Roasted in Microwave Ovens', *Journal of Food Science*, Vol. 50 (1985)
2. Professor Alan Linton – letter to the author, 19 August 1988.
3. 1987 figures from PHLS Food Hygiene Laboratory, Colindale, London.
4. 'Salmonella enteritidis Phage Type 4: Chicken and Egg', *The Lancet* 24 September 1988.
5. 'Salmonella enteritidis phage type 4 infection: association with hens' eggs', *The Lancet* 3 December 1988.
6. P. A. Chapman, P. Rhodes and Wendy Rylands; *Salmonella typhimurium* phage type 141 infections in Sheffield during 1984 and 1985: association with hens' eggs. (*Epidem. Inf.* 1988, 101, pp. 75–82).
7. Wallace E. Garthright, Douglas L. Archer, John E. Kvenberg; *Estimates of Incidence and Costs of Intestinal Infectious Diseases in the United States, Public Health Reports*, March-April 1988, Vol. 103, No. 2 107.
8. 'Poultry-Borne salmonellosis in Scotland'; *Epidem. Inf.* (1988), 101.
9. James H. Steels; 'World Epidemiology of Salmonellosis,' *Int. J. Zoon.*, 10; 45–52, 1983.
10. See n. 8
11. *Farmers Weekly* 1 November 1985.
12. Michael P. Doyle; *Food-Borne Pathogens of Recent Concern* (The Food Research Institute, University of Wisconsin, Madison, Wisconsin, 1985)
13. M. B. Skirrow, 'Campylobacter enteritis – the first five years' *J. Hyg., Camb* (1982)
14. Martin J. Blaser, David N. Taylor and Roger A. Feldman; 'Epidemiology of Campylobacter Jejuni infections', *Epidemiologic Reviews*, Vol. 5, 1983 (The Johns Hopkins University School of Hygiene and Public Health)
15. 'Campylobacter enteritis at a University: Transmission from eating chicken and from cats', *Amer J. Epidemiology*, Vol. 126, No.3.
16. Lisa M Ackerley and Alan Jones; 'Food Poisioning – Fact or Fiction?' *J. Int. Med. Res.* (1985) 13,241
17. As n. 16
18. As n. 14
19. As n. 16
20. As n. 8
21. As n. 13
22. As n. 14
23. *Current Review*, 1 March 1988 (Bureau of Microbial Hazards, Food Directorate, and Bureau of Communicable Disease Epidemiology. Ottawa)
24. David W. Hird; 'Review of Evidence for Zoonotic Listeriosis', *Journal of Food Protection*, Vol. 50, No. 5 (May 1987)

25   W. Kwantes and M. Isaac, 'Listeria Infection in West Glamorgan', In M. Woodbine (ed.), *Problems of Listeriosis*, pp. 112–114 (1975).
26   Letter to *The Lancet*, 12 November 1988 from K. G. Kerr, S. F. Dealler, R. W. Lacey, Dept. of Microbiology, University of Leeds.
27   WHO, Geneva, 1988
28   Telephone conversation with the author, December 1988.
29   Jeffrey M. Farber and Joe Z. Losos; 'Listeria monocytogenes: a food-borne pathogen', *Current Review*, CMAJ, Vol. 138, 1 March 1988.
30   *New Scientist*, 21 July 1988
31   *Ibidem*
32   *The Veterinary Record*, 23 October 1976
33   P. N. Pini and R. J. Gilbert 'The Occurrence in the U.K. of Listeria species in raw chickens and soft cheeses', International Journal of Food Microbiology, No. 6, (1988)
34   As n. 24
35   Letter to the author, 19 August 1988
36   *The Veterinary Record*, 24/31 December 1983
37   G. S. Coutts *Poultry Diseases under Modern Management* (Nimrod Press Ltd., 1987)
38   As n. 37

CHAPTER 6: A BETTER FUTURE

1   Memoranda submitted by RSPCA. First Report from the House of Commons Agriculture Committee, Session 1980–81, Vol. II, p. 141
2   First Report from the House of Commons Agricultural Committee, Session 1980–81, Vol. I, Chapter VI p. 45.
3   Statement by the Archbishop of Canterbury on Animal Welfare Matters, January 1981.
4   The Farm Animal Welfare Council; *Background notes on the Council and its work*.
5   The Farm Animal Welfare Council; *Egg Production Systems – an Assessment*. September 1986.
6   Simmonds Report on Animal Welfare Policy (Doc. AZ–211/86)
7   *Farmers' Guardian*, 27 May 1988.
8   *Poultry World*, September 1987.
9   Sir Richard Body, MP. *Red or Green for Farmers (and the rest of us)*, p 34. Broad Leys Publishing.
10 1987 Survey into the sale of eggs at retail level by Birmingham Trading Standards Officers.
11 Letter to Chickens' Lib from Dr. A. J. Ballantyne, Deputy Director-Poultry at MAFF's Gleadthorpe Experimental Husbandry Farm, 7 September 1988.
12 *Poultry World*, July 1988.
13 *Ibidem*
14 *Ibidem*
15 *Ibidem*

16 *Poultry World*, 26 August 1982.
17 Peter Curtis; *Poultry Diseases, Short Notes Containing Strategic Information for Veterinary Students* (Liverpool University Press.)
18 Letter to Chickens' Lib, 19 June 1985.
19 BEIS press information, 30 September 1988.
20 Letter to Chickens' Lib from Donald Thompson, 27 October 1987.
21 Letter to *The Lancet*, 12 November 1988, from Ildefonso Perales and Ana Audicana, Public Health Laboratory, Basque Government, Bilbao, Spain.

GREEN
P R I N T

GREEN PRINT is an imprint of the Merlin Press, addressing issues raised by the green and environmental movements. Our early titles have included:

LIVING WITHOUT CRUELTY by Mark Gold
THE RACE FOR RICHES by Jeremy Seabrook
THE STOLEN FUTURE by Patrick Rivers
INTO THE 21ST CENTURY edited by Felix Dodds
FAR FROM PARADISE by John Seymour and Herbert Girardet
AFTER THE CRASH by Guy Dauncey
DEVELOPED TO DEATH by Ted Trainer
THE GREEN GUIDE TO ENGLAND by John Button
THE VEGETARIAN HOLIDAY AND RESTAURANT GUIDE by Peter and Pauline Davies
C FOR CHEMICALS by Michael Birkin and Brian Price
CHICKEN AND EGG by Clare Druce

All royalties from our colour cookery book, THE CELEBRITY VEGETARIAN COOKBOOK, edited by Geoff Francis and Janet Hunt, go to the Sarvodaya leaf protein project in Sri Lanka.

Green Print books are available from any bookshop, or from the publishers. If you have difficulty obtaining our books, please let us know. For a catalogue, and to join our free mailing list, write to **Green Print (ML), The Merlin Press, 10 Malden Road, London NW5 3HR.** We'll be glad to hear from you, and to know what you think of our books.